Endorsements:

CW00719875

This is a powerful love story
Precious, and a not so white ¦
against a sharply described backdrop of racists' bigotry,
changing society and outdated, cruel traditions.

We follow Precious's tough journey to bring hope and
joy to the lives of kids on a south London estate. Adrian is a
journalist covering her story, falls in love with her, and so he
begins an adventure taking him places he's never been.

An engaging read, in a style simple, direct, and unadorned,
(Sylvia is a newspaper journalist) but this does not detract
from the deeper message of this story, most appropriately
titled *Not so Black and White*...

kOrky Paul
Zimbabwean born illustrator

Determined to make the most of her life and abilities, Precious
Mukosi swaps rural Kenya for cosmopolitan London, only to
find her new home as tribal as the one she left behind. *Not
So Black and White* is a personal journey and a love story
and a fable of modern living. Precious becomes embroiled
in family feuds, gang wars, a courtroom drama and much
more. Themes of racial, sexual and class prejudice are finely
woven through the story – to great effect. Ultimately, this is
an uplifting story where justice and love win through. An
intricate tale simply told, it's a great read for teenagers and
young adults.

DAI RICHARDS
Well-travelled, documentary film-maker

The story of Precious weaves together the personal and the
political, one woman's extraordinary achievement and the
broad reality of the world we live in. Precious starts out
by helping herself and ends up helping two nations and

hundreds of kids. It is inspired by Nancy Mudenyo Hunt's life experience, which astonishingly has gone from being the poor daughter of a rural chief in Kenya to a winner of the NatWest Most Inspirational Woman award. This gripping and touching novel has well drawn characters. The slow and frustrating experience of turning around a sink-hole estate is recounted without flinching, and the love story between Precious and Adrian is glorious.

KATIE ISBESTER
Publisher- CEO of Claret Press and Claret and Conversation

A heart-warming read that draws out the common humanity that lies beyond differences of nationality, culture, race or class.

DR HALCYON LEONARD
Kenyan born palliative care doctor and GP)

This book is a true page turner. As a librarian I recommend that *Not so Black and White* should be on the reading list of everyone over the age of 14! It is a beautifully written eye opener - a brilliant example of how real life should be written in fiction. What I love about it is that it doesn't down play difficulties but it shows that you don't have to be shackled by your past. You can hope to change your own life and change the world for the better.

DOMINIQUE HENDERSON
Oxfordshire village librarian born in a multi-cultural suburb of Paris - a bit like the Wentworth Estate

A beautiful and fascinating portrayal of how those living completely different lives on opposite sides of the world can come together to change lives. I am incredibly fortunate to call Nancy my friend and to have been a part of the events inspiring this book. Kenya will always have my heart. The creation of Precious Mukosi who drives the plot is a tour de force.

PC LOUISE RUSSELL
Co-founder of Exit 7

I have just finished your book and I loved it. You wouldn't know, but that was the first book I've ever read. I'm a slow reader because of dyslexia. But I found this so easy to read because I could relate to it. Massive congratulations.

PC JOHN CORNELIUS
Co -founder Exit 7

The life story of Precious, the unwanted daughter of a Kenyan chief is a compelling tale of love and gritty determination. I was taken on the challenging journey between the harsh city housing developments of London to the Kenyan village of her birth. Precious is set upon creating a cultural exchange between a dispossessed British urban youth and her Kenyan village, where people appreciate and value the support offered. This book made me feel excited by its potential to create change and make the world a better place.

POLLY BISWAS GLADWIN
Screen-writer and teacher. Polly has set up community film projects in workshops and prisons.

A wonderful novel showing how positive determination in life can overcome cultures and differences to make a 'girl child', a pearl.

DANIEL SHILULI
Teacher in Mumias, Kenya

This is an important piece of writing which shouldn't be missed. Readers from teenagers onwards should find it interesting and thought provoking.

JENNY FORDER

Retired head-teacher UK

It's amazing! The mix of commentary on society and the key message that our differences and experiences can unite us are so important and will definitely have an impact on the people who read it.

KEZIAH BUSS

Sixth former

The character of Precious rose up like the silhouettes of the Acacia trees out of the African savannah and I enjoyed the back and forth between London and Kenya immensely.

LUCY ARTUS

Nasio volunteer and supporter

'Not so Black and White' is a fascinating book which looks at the cross-cultural life of an inspiring young woman Precious, caught between two worlds of the UK and Kenya. The authors manage to weave these worlds together in a proactive way that challenges the reader to take a fresh look at critical issues that are of huge importance in our world today. From gang violence and racial tension in London to arranged marriages, girl child education, and tribal expectations in Kenya. An uplifting and captivating read.

REV'D CHARLOTTE BANNISTER-PARKER

Associate Chaplain to the Bishop of Oxford, Associate Minister, The University Church, Visiting Research Fellow, St Benets, Oxford.

NOT
SO
BLACK AND
WHITE

Nancy Mudenyo Hunt
Sylvia Vetta

'Of all the wonders I have yet heard,
It seems to me most strange that men should fear,
Seeing that Death, a necessary end,
Will come when it will come.'

Nelson Mandela quoting Shakespeare
to Trevor MacDonald

Not so Black and White
Nancy Mudenyo Hunt and Sylvia Vetta 2020

First published in Great Britain 2020 by The Nasio Trust

ISBN 978-0-995543-51-5
ISBN 978-1-910779-61-3 (ePub)

Cover Illustration by Petya Tsankova
Produced by Oxford eBooks

Published by The Nasio Trust

All profits to
The Nasio Trust.
www.thenasiotrust.org

Contents

'In the heart of the British Empire there is a police state where the rule of law has broken down, where murder and torture of Africans by Europeans goes unpunished and where authorities pledged to enforce justice regularly connive at its violation.'

Barbara Castle MP Tribune Sep 30.1955.
Barbara became a cabinet minister in the government of
Harold Wilson.

Prologue
(London June 2019)

Thank you for the update Sis. I send you a (smiling emoji) of satisfaction. When I left Kenya the vulnerability of even a well- educated woman like me was oppressive. Do you remember how I wanted to be a super hero like Wangari Maathai and champion women? That is what you dear sister are becoming – a super hero.

Wangari said that to plant a tree you don't need government permission. That planting just one tree empowers the individual.

The first 'tree' I planted was in London and it felt like seeding hope when I felt despair. The funeral of our father was different. It was about handing over to the next generation.

Don't give up: the young people particularly the girls you are training are going to determine their own future.

Keep strong.
Love from London
Precious

Part 1:
London September 2014

Chapter 1: Wentworth Estate
'What do you expect me to do, Darrel?'

Precious shook her braids in dismay. 'They won't listen to an African.'

'I know these boys. I've watched them grow up. They're not bad. Neglect makes them easy prey. The estate is getting a bad reputation and if we don't stop this downward spiral, even more kids will have their futures blighted.'

Darrel drew in a long slow breath. It wasn't just the kids he had to enthuse and encourage. An insistent tone crept into his voice as he asked her,

'Can we at least try?'

Although she didn't say it, Precious was impressed. Here was a committed young community police officer with a plan. She was moved by Darrel's insight; it was so easy to misinterpret behaviour, but he seemed to understand these kids.

Precious had arrived from Kenya six years ago and had become a leadership and diversity trainer advising the Metropolitan Police, where her different cultural perspective gave her an awareness that a textbook couldn't teach. She had just finished a training seminar where the officers had looked surprised at some of her comments,

'In Africa, children are taught that it's rude to look an adult in the eye but here you think someone looks guilty if they don't look you in the eye.'

The session over PC Darrel Daley had approached her asking for her help on the Wentworth estate. He was persuasive so despite a demanding schedule she relented.

'Okay I'll come to the youth club on Thursday.'

∞

As she headed for the run-down community centre, Precious at first lost her way in the maze that was the estate. The concrete paths were cracked and green with mould and where they were narrow they acted like a wind tunnel. A sudden blast sent litter flying from an over full bin. She heard the clank of metal on brick before turning the corner and seeing a group of boys kicking empty cans against a wall. Precious was not expecting the sharp lash on her cheek. One of the jagged-edged tins rebounded and caught her low on her face. The cut stung fiercely. She grimaced in pain but she didn't shout at them. She knew it was an accident. Besides that, they'd already legged it.

Entering the hall, the teenagers pointed to the bleeding cut.

'What happened to you miss?' asked a small boy with a West African accent.

'I got in the way of a game,' she replied.

Without his policeman's helmet on she saw Darrel's mop of red hair before she saw the rest of him. He looked concerned.

'You should put some antiseptic on that. We've got a first aid kit in the kitchen.'

As she followed him, she commented, 'That lad doesn't look like much of a tearaway to me.'

'That's because he isn't. We don't need to worry about Abeo. He's driven—a hard worker. He'll go far, but he's one of the lucky ones; he's got supportive parents. The young people at the youth club aren't the ones I'm worried about. It's those boys who cut your cheek who're at risk.'

After the cut was dressed, he took her on a tour of the vandalised litter-strewn estate. They soon passed a doorway where Darrel said 'Hello Dan' to a young white man sat on a pile of sleeping bags, stroking his long eared mongrel dog.

A couple who looked Middle Eastern carrying bags of shopping stood aside to let them pass.

'They look like newcomers. I should've introduced myself. Wentworth is one of the estates used to house refugees once they have their status accepted. Some are traumatised. They don't recognise it as post-traumatic stress disorder because getting from one day to the next takes so much effort.'

A girl passed them without looking up. She was engrossed in the music coming from her headphones and seemed to be looking at her feet as she tried out dance steps. Precious stopped and turned, watching her continue up the road, moving to the unheard music. She looked free from worry or cares.

'I've got an idea. Why don't we start with the refugees and asylum seekers? We could use their music as a way for them to reconnect with their country and culture, and it would help them to forget about the stresses of their lives in London,' suggested Precious.

'Sounds like a great idea to me,' said Darrel looking pleased.

Chapter 2: Beginnings
Spices, songs and stories

Precious and Darrel waited to see if anyone would turn up for their first Music Café in the community centre. They carefully avoided looking at the clock, refusing to count the passing minutes and tried not to let the dingy green peeling paintwork depress them. When five people came through the door they smiled with relief. Three of them had brought musical instruments.

'What's that?' asked Darrel resisting the urge to touch the highly polished wood of an instrument carried by a young woman wearing a hijab.

'It's a lute,' said the Iranian woman.

Precious allowed herself to relax, asked her name and encouraged her to talk about the instrument. After that it was easy to persuade the musician to begin. The atmosphere changed: the room echoed with the sound of mournful but haunting songs. Precious asked the Pakistani man with his tabla whether he could accompany Delaram if she played a couple of verses again. At first, his rhythms on the hand drums were hesitant but, as they adapted and connected through music, by the end they were both delighted. The Bosnian violinist began slowly then faster and faster played an energetic dance but looked disappointed that there was no one to dance to the sounds of his homeland.

Precious served Middle Eastern savoury snacks and chocolate biscuits. Over tea, she thanked the musicians and said

'If we organise the café again next month, do you have any friends you can bring with you? We need your help to spread the word that this café is for everyone wherever they come from.'

The next meeting, Precious and Darrel once again sat nervously in the community centre silently waiting for the musicians. Once again, the minutes ticked by. And once again, they smiled in relief when their little group arrived, this time joined by a company of Africans.

Their upbeat singing made an enormous difference, grabbing the attention of passers-by who put their heads around the open door. They were surprised to hear the vibrant sound of Africa accompanied by instrumentalists from Asia and Eastern Europe adapting to the rhythms. Some tried to avoid eye contact and hurried on but others couldn't stop themselves smiling. The singers moving forward swaying rhythmically and drew in the onlookers.

Precious saw this as a possible breakthrough and beckoned them in to join in the dancing. At first people seemed shy, but then one by one they took to the floor. Half an hour later she surveyed the now crowded room. There were residents from most backgrounds around the world save one: Afro-Caribbean. She had heard stories interpreted by Africans as hostility towards them by some in the Afro-Caribbean community. A flicker of sadness in her eyes she asked Darrel,

'Do you think it's because I'm African that they are staying away?'

'I really don't know, Precious.'

∞

When she'd fled Kenya, it had been easy for Precious to engage with other Africans but she had found it difficult to connect in a meaningful way with English people. That changed when she made a friend through church. Katie was the first white person to invite her home and they found they had a lot in common. Precious was able to share her thoughts with Katie without fear of judgement.

She set off for the fifth floor flat in Vauxhall not far from the hospital where Katie worked as a nurse. Her friend gave her a warm welcome and put the kettle on. Precious laughed as she said, 'You're turning me into an Englishwoman, only the colour of your tea.'

As Katie filled their mugs, Precious told her about the Wentworth Estate. Her friend brushed her curly brown hair off her face and settled down to listen.

'Katie, have you any idea how I can engage some of the teenagers? They seem so apathetic as if it's not cool to be enthusiastic about anything.'

Katie stared at her tea, not saying anything. Then she got to her feet and tidied up their mugs and some dishes. Precious watched her. Finally, Katie sat back down, a resolution clearly written on her face.

'Let's dress up and go to a club in Brixton and see what kind of music teenagers like and you could try to provide that on the estate?

∞

With her new found insights into current musical tastes among the young club goers, Precious approached the gang who had accidently injured her. The residents regarded them as a nuisance although the language they used was more colourful. 'Pain in the arse' being the nicest of the expressions. She tried to enthuse them with the club music idea but it left them cold. Disappointed, she walked away but noticed them wave to an old lady who responded with a warm smile.

She described the encounter to Darrel.

'That's Icolyn,' he said. 'She's amazing. She's seventy-seven and runs the soup kitchen. Every Wednesday she and her friends cook for fifty homeless people. Word's got around that her roast dinners would grace The Ivy.'

'Let's get her advice,' suggested Precious.

∞

The walls of Icolyn's flat were covered with photographs of her children and grandchildren. While they talked, her eye was drawn to a wedding photograph.

'Henry was a good man—a real grafter. I still miss him,' Icolyn said, noticing the photo holding Precious's attention. 'Life was hard for me when he died. I needed three jobs to support the family.'

'That must be why you're so empathetic. You know how hard times can arrive when you're least expecting them.'

'What is it you want to know?' asked Icolyn, 'I'm sure you aren't just here to lay on the complements but I'd be a lying if I say I didn't enjoy it.'

'Can you start by telling me a bit more about yourself, please?'

'I grew up in rural Jamaica. We didn't have electricity, but we had good food. My mother, she create wonders with the fruit and vegetables we grew. My parents were subsistence farmers. Rice was tough to grow—my father struggled with that and we never had any to sell. I looked after the pigs and goats and wandered freely. Children round here—a lot don't know what good fresh food and air is.'

'Would you help us teach them?' asked Precious.

∞

The next year was a complete whirlwind as the Wentworth estate started to transform into a more hopeful place where young people were encouraged to respect themselves. Once their self- image changed Darrel, Precious and Icolyn tried planting seeds of ambition.

The change began with Icolyn's cooking lessons. Precious was surprised that promise of food lured the boys where music had failed. She was impressed by the respect that

Icolyn had gained from lads whose preferred stance was fortress-like. She mused that the attraction could be the non-judgemental warmth that Icolyn radiated.

On the first day of the class, they walked through the door with a determined casualness making sure their presence was felt. Icolyn was not intimidated, but beckoned to them.

'I need your help. Chop those vegetables for me. Yes, that's what a knife's intended for. You boys will turn my grey hair white with worry.'

'Don't you worry, Ma. We can look after ourselves.'

'That's what I'm worried about!' Icolyn joked back.

She became their warm and caring grandmother. The muscular lads strutted and bragged, but underneath they craved love. She taught them to make soups and smoothies, which they served to the music lovers. Doing something useful, they became appreciated. One of the boys did a high five with Icolyn after adults started to greet them on the street.

'Get me, Ma. I swear we be looking decent, too much decent Ma.'

The boys even agreed to collect just over the best-before date produce from the nearby supermarkets, so they could provide meals for kids after school.

'Good work, boys. That food is perfectly edible, no point it going in the bin.' Icolyn nodded approvingly, when the boys showed her their donations.

The aromas wafting from the community centre kitchen were hard to identify. Some residents prepared recipes from their home countries and shared their knowledge of spices, taking pleasure in passing on their insight to the next generation. The free food lured in more and more people. Over a meal they got to know neighbours who had been strangers, creating conversation and a sense of belonging.

But Icolyn didn't stop there. She asked her son Euton and

his brother to organise discos on Friday nights. They looked at the dismal hall in despair.

'Come on, Ma. You want us to lime here? This place is so not cool.'

Her look of disappointment galvanised Euton.

'Chillax, Ma. Don't fret yourself. We'll sort it.'

Somehow, they cajoled their friends into joining a decorating party. To the accompaniment of reggae and the allure of Icolyn's cooking, they transformed the centre into a colourful welcoming space. They started regular discos and used the money raised to modernise the kitchen. No longer to be avoided, the community centre became a place where people of all cultures were happy to be seen.

But a hard core of teenagers appeared impenetrable.

'Could sport entice them?' suggested Darrel. They agreed it was worth a try.

There were no playing fields within walking distance. The bleak litter-strewn concrete square at the heart of the estate was all they had.

He approached Wanderers FC for help. The timing was right. The team were in need of some good publicity in the local community. One of their players had been sent off for what everyone regarded as a racist incident and it had been all over the papers. They helped enable an FA grant to replace the concrete with an all-weather five-a-side pitch with a high wire fence. Two of the players volunteered to coach the boys. News spread about the local celebrities coming to the estate and soon twenty lads, four girls and some dads were turning up.

Precious was astonished by the progress they had made. Week by week, month by month, the Wentworth Estate was becoming a friendlier and more inviting place to live. She was starting to think that her being African wasn't after all such an obstacle. She felt welcome. Everyone breathed the change of atmosphere until there was no problem getting volunteers to come on board the Crossroads Project.

The first challenge for the new board of trustees was a triangle of unloved ground where some young adults left evidence of their activities in the form of cigarette ends, empty cans, crisp packets and needles. Precious persuaded two of them to join a team interested in creating a community garden. When some of their ideas were adopted, they became enthusiastic. They needed funding to help with the makeover so Precious asked if any of the youth club members could write letter to their local councillor, asking for a small grant.

'But I've never written a letter,' said Emily. 'Could you help?'

Abeo sat down to have a go. Precious looked at him appreciatively.

'Have you done this before?'

'No, Miss but I'm used to doing what my Mum asks me. She has lots to do and expects me to help. If I don't do what she asks first time I'm in trouble.'

'This is voluntary Abeo. I hope it is something you want to do?'

'I love reading Miss. My dream is one day to write a book, a book with someone like me in it. Can you help me miss?'

'I can help you with this letter. I do know what you mean Abeo. I love stories. They take you to another place in another time. I'll see if there are any lessons and groups maybe at the library who can help you? '

Precious and Darrel had already approached the Councillor because each member of the council had access to minor funds that was in their gift for use in their ward. They wanted the youngsters to get the credit so Councillor Abbas invited Emily and Abeo to meet him at the Town Hall. Darrel accompanied them because Precious was working.

They were awestruck going through the large doors. At

reception Darrel said, 'This is Abeo Amah and Emily Jones for Councillor Abbas.'

'I'll call him.'

A few minutes later the councillor came down the marble staircase and held out a hand for them to shake. The children looked nervous but they relaxed when the Councillor smiled and said, 'My office isn't as impressive as this,' gesturing to the foyer. 'Follow me and once we've talked, how about I show you around and we go for tea or juice and cake in the café?'

Emily and Abeo beamed. When, a week later, they received a letter from Councillor Abbas allotting the project £1000, they were ecstatic.

Work began immediately and Darrel wanted to pinch himself when three of the tougher boys volunteered to help with the physical work. The most enthusiastic helpers were Emily and Abeo. A date was set for the official opening. The news that an EastEnders star had agreed to cut the ribbon sent the estate gossip mill into overdrive.

Chapter 3: Unrest.
Why would they do that?

Precious felt her work was done and that she could indulge in some time for herself. She was happy to remain on the committee and attend events like the garden opening ceremony but after that Darrell and his band of volunteers were perfectly capable of carrying the project forward. She had a demanding day job and even her phenomenal energy was being tried by the volunteering.

On her last day she said her farewells at the youth club and Darrel walked her out. They were turning the corner towards the garden when they froze, rooted to the spot.

'Who would do that and why?' Precious wept as they stared at the destruction.

They stepped unsteadily over the chopped down shrubs covering the path and picked up the trampled flowers. The fence at the end of the garden was daubed with graffiti and there were shards of broken glass scattered over the toddlers' sand pit.

They retraced their steps back to the club and called everyone together.

'Many of you worked hard this summer on the garden makeover. If you know who destroyed your good work, let me know. Please help—here's my number,' said Darrel giving out cards to everyone. 'You can ring me. You don't have to give me your name — just the names of the sick vandals who've done this.'

∞

A week later as she left the tube station, Precious made her way to the Crossroads Project trustees meeting. She wondered if it was possible to repair the garden ready for the official opening and if they did, would it be vandalised again?

'Hi, miss.'

Precious's attention was drawn back to the present as Abeo Amah waved to her. The smiling schoolboy had been the first African child she had met working on the estate two years ago. Unlike many of the boys his age, there was no doubt in Precious's mind that Abeo would go far. She watched for a minute as he skipped and jumped in the direction of the cheerful revamped library. It was Thursday and open late. Seeing him cheered her up — boys like him made all her effort feel worthwhile. She carried on down the road, ready to focus on the meeting.

The everyday life of Kingsdown Road was interrupted by a cry of pain.

An eerie instinct clicked in. Precious turned, almost knowing already what she'd see. A scream penetrated the noise of the traffic. Her scream. 'No!'

She ran flat out towards the library entrance where Abeo was lying on the ground, blood spilling over his school uniform.

Two boys she thought she recognised from the estate were running across the road, swearing. They disappeared down a side road. A young office worker was already on the phone calling for an ambulance. Precious knelt beside Abeo. She took off her scarf and tied it tightly to try and stop the bleeding.

'Stay with me please, Abeo.' She held in him her arms and cradled his head. 'Look at me. Say something. Please talk to me.'

'Miss…' Abeo started to reply and then he was gone. An act of casual violence that lasted just a few seconds had ended Abeo's exuberant life. The ambulance took away his small body. Police closed the library and cordoned off the area.

PC Darrel Daley, who had also been on his way to the meeting, sat beside Precious, too shocked to even speak.

'I could only see their backs as they ran away, Darrel, but I could swear one of them was Nelson Wilson.'

Darrel didn't look surprised. Nelson had been one of the few whom they hadn't been able to reach.

'He's joined the Wolf Crew. It was his gang who vandalised the garden—they wanted to scare others off and continue to deal there.'

'But why would they pick on Abeo?'

'Oh Jeez. Precious, it was Abeo who told me that it was them vandalising the garden.'

'Darrel—his parents! They think he's studying in the library.'

Darrel went across to the inspector and five minutes later returned to Precious.

'I've told them about Nelson and suggested they also look for Jacob Morris. He and Nelson have been running around together a lot lately. I'm sorry, Precious, but they need you to go to the station to make a statement, and they want to know if they can have your coat.' He pointed to the bloodstains.

Precious took it off and Darrel handed it to another officer, who bagged it up and labelled it.

'I wish you could come with me to break the news to his parents, but you're the chief witness and the police want you to go with them now.'

Darrel's expression spoke loud and clear—this was the worst job he'd ever had to do. 'Just one minute. I need to phone Councillor Abbas. I'll let him know what's happened and that we won't make the meeting.'

As Precious left with Inspector Ball for a formal interview, her head was pounding. She tried hard to think clearly. As she got into the police car, she recognised a group of Somali boys on the opposite side of the road. She sighed. Had all her work been for nothing? Had Nelson and his gang been hunting down the Somalis when they encroached on their patch.

∞

Darrel headed for Mitchel Tower. It was a depressing place at the best of times with soulless landings and stairways tagged with graffiti and – not the kind by Banksy. Today it was even worse because the lifts were out of order. At least the Amahs lived on the fifth floor, not the eighteenth. He climbed the stairs with slow and heavy steps under flickering fluorescent tubes. If he could have taken the lift, he wouldn't have had time to over think. His training had taught him how to pass on unwelcome news. The most traumatic experience in his career had been a road traffic collision when he'd had to tell the grandparents about their son's injury and the death of their granddaughter.

Abeo's death felt different to Darrel. He felt like he'd personally failed the young boy. His rational self knew it wasn't his fault, but he was the face of law on the estate. Why had he asked the youth club members to inform on the vandals? Recruiting Precious had made a difference but now this. This had quickly become the worst assignment he'd ever had, and as he climbed the five floors of stairs he was tempted to drag his feet.

Grace Amah was wearing her carer's uniform when she opened the door to their flat. As soon as she saw Darrel in his uniform she looked around for Abeo.

'What's the boy done?' she shouted. Joshua Amah joined them.

'Is this about Abeo? Has he done something wrong?' he asked, genuinely perplexed.

Darrel replied, 'No, Mr and Mrs Amah. Abeo has not done anything wrong. Please, may I come in?

He was ushered into a sparsely furnished, but spotlessly clean, living room.

'It might be best if you sat down,' he suggested.

Grace and Joshua sat with their hands clenched. Their expressions showed that they expected this wouldn't be good news, but they were not prepared for Darrel's words.

'I'm so sorry, Mr and Mrs Amah. I hate to be the bearer of bad news. Abeo was stabbed outside the library. He has been taken to St Thomas'.'

'He'll be alright though, won't he? It's a good hospital. I'll get my coat. I want to be with him,' said Grace as she stood up.

'Please, Mrs Amah? Please sit down. I don't know how to tell you this. Abeo won't be coming home. He died outside the library.'

Joshua and Grace looked at each other in shock.

'How can I tell our family?' Grace whispered. Darrel was taken aback by her pragmatic reaction, and started to speak again, not sure if they had understood him. But before he could say anything Grace's face crumpled and a sound of anguish began like a whimper, but became louder and louder as tears rolled freely down her face. Grace waved her arms frantically above her head, screamed and ran out of the room. Joshua excused himself and followed her into the bedroom shutting the door behind him.

Darrel heard painful sounds like someone banging their head against a wall. Then Joshua's deep voice trying to calm his wife.

'Grace, please. I need you. I don't want to lose you too.'

Another piercing scream was followed by heart-rending sobs. Ten minutes later, they returned to the lounge.

'We would like to see our son,' said Grace using all her strength of will to hold back the tears.

'I'll take you there. It's the hardest thing for a parent to do.

But we need you to identify him.'

'Who did this?' asked Joshua.

'It's too early to say what happened but we will do our best to find the perpetrators and bring them to justice. The incident happened in public and we have witnesses. We'll look at the CCTV cameras. I promise we won't leave any stone unturned.'

'Why didn't we take it seriously, Joshua? He tried to tell us,' Grace kept repeating,

'Tell you what? Please, Mrs Amah. It may help us find and prosecute his killers,' said Darrel.

'Dear Lord. Why, Joshua? Why did we come here?' she shouted. Joshua looked at Darrel.

'We're from Ghana,' said Joshua.

'You may not have known but Abeo had a health problem. When he was four years old he started to have fits. It took every penny we had to bring him to this country. We thought he would have a better future here, good treatment and a good education. His fits were brought under control but he has to be careful—no rugby or boxing. But he doesn't mind. Everything he loves he finds in books and music. That's why he loves the library. I feel proud when I hear the librarians praise him…' Joshua stopped. 'I'm talking about him as if he's… I won't believe he's gone unless I see for myself. There's been a mistake. It is NOT Abeo. Let's go.'

'Of course. We can talk later,' said Darrel.

While the Amahs got ready to leave, Darrel phoned Councillor Abbas at the trustees meeting to warn them.

'It's been a long time since something like this happened here. We don't want it to undo the good you've done. Do what you can to keep tempers under control.'

∞

It felt strange sitting opposite Inspector Ball. He had been on

31

the interviewing panel that had appointed her. She had been driven to apply for the post by a racist incident, in which the police's perfunctory behaviour showed they had no idea how it felt to be on the receiving end. At that interview she'd made a point of coming across as a leader. She had to in the male-dominated world of the police force. This felt so different. She didn't feel strong now. A wave of helplessness swept over her.

'You said they were swearing. Did you hear what they said?' said Inspector Ball.

'As they ran across the road they said, 'Stupid motherfucking African shit.' I heard the 'African shit' quite clearly, but I can't swear to the 'stupid'. It could have been *sucks.*' Precious answered.

'Are you saying that he may have been stabbed because he was African?'

Precious nodded.

'Constable Daley told me that Abeo had reported Nelson Wilson and the Wolf Crew for vandalising the community garden. It's a problem on the estate. The Wolf Crew are of Afro Caribbean ancestry and they have taken against the Africans. That could have been the reason but maybe there's more to it, or he was just in the wrong place at the wrong time.

'I'm sorry, Sir. I've told you everything I saw that could be of help in the investigation.'

'I'll get your statement typed up,' he replied. 'Go home, get some sleep. Come back here in the morning to check it and sign it. Let me know immediately if you remember anything else that could be useful.'

∞

Precious unlocked the door of her one-bedroom apartment. She felt dirty. She needed to wash away the day, to wash away the sight of blood and the hate and the tragedy.

She eventually emerged in a pristine white bathrobe with a towel turban on her head and fell on the bed, feeling the desperation in her body. It was as if she had fallen in a poisonous river. She was alone with no-one to draw out the toxin. Exhausted she fell asleep but spent a restless night tossing around in a state of half consciousness. All the while a white noise throbbed in her head.

She dreamed of Croesus, or was it Midas weighing his gold? Suddenly Midas had the face of her father and was forcing her onto the scales. She felt a great sense of betrayal as she realised what he was doing. He was putting a price on her in Kenyan shilling, goats, sheep and cattle. She was not an item of property. She was Precious Lutta Mukosi and valued her mind more than her possessions, which in any case were few. The men discussing her worth were negotiating to enhance their status not hers. She cried at the thought of leaving her mother and the humiliation it would bring on her family, but a stronger force was driving her to find a way to escape from this arranged marriage. Her whole being was consumed by a desire to run away.

Perspiration dripped off her in cold old England. Seven years had passed since she'd felt that overwhelming desire to flee Kenya as she watched her father negotiate her bride price. Without warning that longing for flight returned. She'd been working with the police for nearly six years and seen distressing domestic violence but not felt like this before. Why had this murder touched her so deeply?

Chapter 4: Reporting
Adrian Harris from the Wentworth Estate

'The police are doing their best, but they lack the resources to create sustainable change. Young people are carrying knives because they are angry or because they feel unsafe. The volume of drugs in the area is fuelling gang battles and there is less police funding. It's a deadly mix. To make things even more complicated, many of the young people in the gangs have mental health issues.'

Adrian was hearing the same story from everyone he interviewed for the *London Post*. They stressed different ingredients but the results were similar; some young people engaged in a strange tribalism, often determined by postcode. When a Somali gang encroached on the area claimed by the Afro-Caribbean Wolf Crew, they took it as seriously as if Germany had invaded Belgium. Parents on the estate lost their smiles. On edge, most were reluctant, even afraid, to talk to reporters.

'I'm worried that Crossroads' good work will be unravelled if we can't heal the rift between young people from Afro-Caribbean and African backgrounds,' said Councillor Abbas. 'It could spill over and affect parents who live side by side with a degree of tolerance but also some suspicion. Let's hope this is a one-off case. We must do all we can to contain the situation.'

The following morning Adrian was surprised to see his report on the front page. He was inundated with emails and phone calls inviting him to be interviewed on the radio. The invitation to a discussion on knife crime on Newsnight was more than unexpected.

It was Adrian's first experience on the other side of the camera. His palms were sweaty and his throat dry as the lights went up and he felt exposed in a way he didn't with his print journalism. Angela Mantel began her opening about Abeo's murder. When she was finished, she turned to him.

'Could there be a particular reason that this murder happened on the Wentworth Estate area, and are young African and Afro-Caribbean men disproportionately represented in the gangs operating there?'

He took a deep breath and began, 'According to most studies, Afro-Caribbean boys start well in school but some of them, particularly from troubled backgrounds, get excluded from secondary school and get drawn into drugs and gangs. We know there are men in their twenties and thirties who regard themselves as 'Law Lords' who prey on these boys' vulnerability. It's a form of grooming. East, West and South African ancestry children are among the best educational performers and don't tend to join gangs, but there are gangs of Somali ancestry.'

There was a fellow guest, Precious Mukosi, but he was told that she couldn't comment on the murder. Mantel asked her to describe the transformative work of the Crossroads Project.

'Conditions on the estate had improved and violence reduced remarkably over the past two years. Please don't judge everyone on the estate by this terrible event,' pleaded Precious, her large dark eyes sad and sincere.

'Most African families, like Abeo's parents, are determined to invest everything in a good education for their children. Many African children have fled wars or terrible family circumstances and see academic success as their way out of poverty. It's as if the African children's hunger and love of learning is seen as a threat to some gang members.'

Adrian hung back after the interview, waiting to see if he could catch the engaging Kenyan who'd spoken so directly on national television. After twenty minutes, he was forced to give up—he had deadlines at the paper that needed his attention.

∞

The London Post's curiosity was aroused. Who was this African woman and what was she doing working on a troubled estate in London? Why had they never heard of her before? Following the success of his last article on Wentworth, the editor asked Adrian to write an in-depth feature on Precious and Crossroads.

In his fifteen years' experience as a journalist he had encountered bizarre and even menacing interviews, but no reply astonished him quite so much as the answer Precious gave to a simple question.

Adrian was well prepared for the interview. He'd learned that she'd arrived in England in 2005 to read for a Masters in Change Management at Westminster University. It appeared that she'd lived and worked at a women's refuge while studying to pay her way.

He asked her why she'd taken on such an emotionally taxing role while also completing a Masters. She told him that she'd wanted the chance to support and empower women who were fleeing domestic abuse.

He guessed the job offered free accommodation. After so long working on a newspaper, Adrian had become cynical about human nature. Precious carried on unaware of this.

'I was amazed that English women were victims. When I arrived in the UK, I thought this was an African problem, but now I believe it's universal. Did you know that during the football season in England, the volume of domestic violence incidences rises? They call it the "Stella Artois effect" caused by the "wife beaters beer".'

He wondered if she could be an insomniac, working long hours while being a full-time student. But the tall elegant woman with the immaculate braided hair and expression of confidence and pride didn't appear to be ravaged by sleepless nights. He'd found nothing online about her background in Kenya which was why he decided to ask her the simplest and, it transpired, the most surprising question.

'Tell me where were you born?

'I was born in Tusanda in West Kenya,' she replied in a beautifully modulated voice.

'And when was that?' he asked peering over his glasses hoping she wasn't one of those women who hated giving her age.

She raised her sculpted eyebrows and looked straight at him.

'I have no idea,' was the startling reply.

Seeing his look of confusion, Precious took pity on Adrian and explained. 'My father was the tribal chief and like your Henry VIII he was desperate for a son. I was his fourth daughter. Not only did he walk away in disgust without acknowledging my existence – he didn't even register my birth. Imagine my mother's distress. He was grieving for a recently lost brother, and she wanted to placate him by naming me after my Uncle Lutta. Mosi, my oldest sister, was horrified that I had a male name and no birth certificate. When she became an adult, she rectified the omission. When registering my birth, she gave me my female name Precious. That's why I am Precious Lutta Mukosi. Sadly, Mosi died when I was eight years old, and no one has any idea whether the date she recorded was my real date of birth or one she made up.'

Adrian's hazel eyes peered over his glasses looking straight at Precious and he spoke in a kind voice.

'Given such an unpromising start what do you think accounts for your success? Do you think that eight-year-old girl would look at me in disbelief if I'd said she'd become a distinguished trainer in the Metropolitan Police, who would change the lives of hundreds of disadvantaged young people? Could she have even pictured the Wentworth housing estate, given her surroundings?'

The strong face in front of him dissolved in tears. Shaken, Adrian put out his hand to touch hers. She drew it away so suddenly that he knew he must have crossed a line. She left the room hurriedly, muttering, 'Excuse me a moment.'

Precious returned a few minutes later, tissue in hand but nonetheless composed.

'I'm so sorry about that. The way you described that little girl… How a privileged white man—a graduate of the London School of Economics—could picture that child shook me.' She laughed at the shocked look on his face. 'Yes, I looked you up before agreeing to this interview! I expected we'd be talking about the project. This is the first time I've talked to anyone about my childhood. I had no idea I'd react like that.'

She paused, deep in thought finally adding,

'It's as if you have given me permission to look at my past. Because I came here alone and built a life here alone, I like to think that I am strong. I hate to admit it but I'm feeling a bit vulnerable after getting abusive tweets after that Newsnight interview. Your question took me back to a time when I was at the mercy of misogynistic traditions.'

Unsettled by her remarks, Adrian took time before he replied and made an uncharacteristic offer.

'Editors hate us showing our features to the interviewee before publication, but given what you've just said, why not relive that childhood? I'll send you the copy and if there is anything you don't want to see in print, you can delete it. Do you trust me to do that?'

'Actually, I think I do,' admitted Precious.

As she left the interview, Precious felt drained but excited. There was something about Adrian, maybe it was his eyes, maybe his modest sounding voice with its touch of a North London accent that made her feel safe. Growing up, she'd seen her mother and the other women in Tusanda suffer at the hands of men and working in the refuge hadn't helped rectify that image. Like the women she'd met at the refuge who were fleeing abusive husbands, she'd lost trust in men.

Adrian's profile feature was longer than most – a double centre spread and the photographer had taken a dramatic picture of Precious, emphasising her graceful neck, elegant posture and strong features. There was no mention of Abeo. She still couldn't speak about the case before she appeared at the trial. Precious knew it was a legal necessity, but she resented not being able to talk about it. It felt like she had to pretend it hadn't happened.

The rise of knife crime was on the minds of most Londoners. She was confident that Adrian's empathetic and unbiased reporting, which was bringing more readers to the paper, had done a good job at conveying the nuanced dynamics of the situation at Wentworth. Her remarks on Newsnight concerning Africans and Afro-Caribbeans had provoked the accusations of racism. She mulled over the idea of contacting him to get his advice about how to deal with them.

As she sat on the bus on the way home, she thought about how open she'd been with him, and how she'd described the difference between Tusanda and Wentworth. *'My first post working as a civilian with the Metropolitan Police had a bizarre title: Domestic Violence Co-ordinator. That's when I got to know the Wentworth Estate. Compared to an African village the accommodation is luxurious. Continuous electricity, water on demand, good sanitation, modern gadgets and computer games, but it lacks what my village had by the spadeful:*

community spirit. Here, when marriages or partnerships break down, mothers are alone without neighbourly help and need two jobs to maintain their families. They're so exhausted that their teenage sons can get out of hand. It's understandable that under such pressure and without any support, some of them simply give up and turn to drink and drugs for escape. In Tusanda, a child belongs to the whole village, and every adult has the right to punish you if they find you doing something you're not meant to be doing. '

Walking home after the interview Precious felt a frisson of unease. She'd pushed Kenya to the back of her mind for so long, that sharing so many memories with Adrian had been a strange experience. For every warm memory of her mother and sisters, there was a painful memory of her father, of his other wives sneering at her mother and of her male relatives talking down to her. As she slipped her key into the lock and pushed open the door to her flat, she felt calm and reassured and surprisingly at home—a feeling she doubted she would recover if she returned to Tusanda.

Chapter 5: Memories of Kenya
The genie is out of the bottle

The recollections came to her everywhere, when she was at work or on the bus, or on her way back from church or visiting friends. That genie of a journalist had un-bottled suppressed memories and as much as she tried to ward them off by keeping herself busy, they kept flooding back when she least expected them.

∞

The tall, distinguished bald-headed chief, a descendant of the ruling Tanga clan, was well-respected and feared. When her father walked from one homestead to another people bowed down to acknowledge his presence and moved aside to let him through.

His second wife, Mama Murono, had a home surrounded by a thick fence with a narrow red-earthed path leading to the main house. The door faced the large wooden bamboo gate. There were two smaller grass-thatched huts on the left, ready to house third and fourth wives who would produce more desperately wanted sons. Behind the huts were a banana plantation and a few mango trees where her father pottered around carrying a panga[1] . When he'd finished, he'd approach the gate whistling loudly so everyone would know he had arrived.

Mama Murono was large in stature with a big bust. She looked proud as she sat at the entrance of her house, watching whoever approached from the gate. Whenever she heard Kidake's whistling, she relished calling loudly to her son, 'Osundwa, come and say hallo to your father'.

Kioni and Mama Murono were not friends. Precious had

_____
1 a small sharp tool used for cutting overgrowth

often heard her mum complaining that Mama Murono was unkind and enjoyed mocking her for not bearing any sons. Precious remembered one occasion when her mother had answered back. She'd watched, helpless, as her father beat her mother and chased her away until she apologised and returned with a chicken to appease the second wife.

Whenever her mother felt low or humiliated, she stretched her long neck in a way that Precious knew was one of her own habits. Kioni recited out aloud, 'I am Kioni, the chief's first wife'—she always emphasised the word 'first'—'and I need to be informed on current affairs to help our village women understand their role and duty to their community and country.'

Tears came to her eyes as Precious remembered one day as a small child. It was of the day she'd asked her father for money to attend school.

'Come here, Precious Lutta. Stop what you are doing. Change out of those dirty clothes and wash your face. Your father is coming. Can you hear him beat his panga on the fence?' Precious's father spent most of his time with his second wife who had given him Osundwa, his first-born son.

Kioni's daughter had already guessed that he was expected. Her mother was cooking a special brown porridge, a traditional staple food made from millet, maize flour and cassava.

'Come and eat, daughter. This is what gives us a full stomach to work on the farm'

As Precious ate her porridge, Kioni took the wind-up radio out of the cupboard. It was a family tradition that she started her day with the morning news and prayers.

Over the tinny sound of the radio Kioni addressed her youngest daughter.

'It's time you went to school, Precious Lutta. You're a smart girl and a fast learner, but you'll soon be five and we need the school fees. Once your father has eaten and looks relaxed, ask him. Make sure you are nice and respectful.'

Precious heard her father at the gate shouting to his second wife about the goat who'd not been given water.

With an intense amount of willpower she lured herself out of the memory and back into the present where she was mindlessly putting away her shopping. She sighed as she realised that she hadn't been concentrating for the last several minutes as she pulled a bunch of bananas out of the bread bin and placed them in the fruit bowl.

Pulling out a chopping board, knife and vegetables, she began preparing her dinner, remembering bitterly how the boys at home had always been served first at mealtimes. It was only after the herd's boys and the other male workers were given food that the women and girls got to eat. Precious's father ate his food in his special place under the big mango tree in the middle of the compound. Uncles and neighbours came to keep him company, inform him of what was going on in the village or seek advice about land disputes.

As the childhood memories dissipated, the more recent recollection of how she opened up to Adrian made Precious bite her lip in embarrassment. Why had she talked to him about her childhood? Why had she told him how the women were treated differently? She should have kept it buried. She had told Adrian a story that was so painful to her. It made her believe her father had no love for her but there were times when he played affectionately with his daughters and that confused her.

'You'll understand how hard it was for me to approach my father when he wasn't under the big mango trees surrounded by men fawning over him. But I plucked up the courage because I was desperate even then for an education. I may not have been able to articulate it, but I knew it was the key to my freedom. So I approached him, as mother had suggested,

43

when he was alone, and I said, "Respected father, do you think I am tall for my age?"

'He laughed and agreed. "People say I am a clever girl. I want you to be proud of me so I'd like to go to school. Mother doesn't have the money but the fee is small. Please, can you give it to her?"

'Father's expression changed, he spat on the ground, a sign that you'd made him angry. I waited, afraid of what he would say next. He dismissed me angrily. "I have enough expense educating your brothers. Go and help your mother in the kitchen."'

Precious covered her mouth, her throat choked with emotion.

'Little did I know that others, including Mama Murono, were peeping through windows to see what was going on. They knew father was never to be approached without permission and were curious about my behaviour.

'As a child I dreamed about getting on a plane to the distant land my dad had described, where it was so clean that the pavements had no dust or mud. When I told my half- sister Aluna about my dream, she laughed and thought it was a big joke.

'There was no way I could get to the Eldorado my father called London but I was a rebellious teenager and, by the age of sixteen, I was concerned about my future. Lots of girls in the village were already married off at that age.'

Adrian had asked her 'How did you get educated?'

'Thanks to my mother, who scrimped and saved to pay for my early schooling. My elder sister Nechesa was better at handling my father. Influenced by her, father's attitude to female education began to change and he wanted me to follow her to university. But he still wanted to control me.

'I had a compelling desire to be free and have an experience of somewhere different – to be helicoptered into a different world. That's why I crossed the border to Uganda. It wasn't far. More of a bus ride away than anything else. But when I came home the next day, my father was so angry with me – girls were not allowed independence. He hit me and then looked shaken that he had raised his hand to me for the first time.'

That was where she had stopped the interview. She had not told Adrian why she had come to England.

Although painful memories of her childhood and the interview kept interrupting her daily life, none were as searing as the nightmares she had about Abeo. Precious felt helpless after witnessing the little boy's murder. She had experienced pain, suffering and anger growing up in Kenya but never before had she witnessed anything close to this: the murder of an innocent boy on the streets of London.

∞

When the feature appeared in *The London Post* she was surprised to see Sergeant Jones reading it.

'It looks like your father knows how to treat women.' He grinned to make it sound like a joke. Her smile in return was more of a twist of her lips, because they both knew it wasn't a joke.

'Congratulations are in order. Really, we sure need good publicity. Well done.' said one of her female colleagues. It was like that all day, emails and phone calls from people who had seen the feature. Precious was not used to that level of praise or publicity.

She decided to email Adrian to thank him and share an idea that she hoped might interest him.

Chapter 6: Demanding Change
Passions and persuasion
London 2016

Community activism hadn't initially appealed to Adrian but Precious was persuasive, so he gave her idea a try. Despite his concern that he'd feel an outsider, he began to enjoy his time on the estate. The monthly community paper he established, the *Wentworth Mirror*, proved popular and the contributions were infused with humour and, to his surprise, poetry. His voluntary work influenced his journalism as he connected with the experiences of people on the estate. In turn, they began to trust him.

Thirty eight year old Adrian had had relationships from time to time but his passion for journalism meant working unsocial hours, which got in the way of romance. Due to the rise of social media, the industry was under intense pressure. Many old friends had been made redundant. His enthusiasm was challenged and an element of disillusion had crept up on him threatening to undermine his vision of himself. He reluctantly admitted to himself that was possibly an excuse on his part. When relationships had started to get serious he'd always backed off. On each occasion he'd had the same phrase flung at him: 'lack of commitment.' At least he was a committed commitment-phobe, he joked to himself.

Precious suggested they attend Icolyn's son Euton's Friday night Caribbean Disco and he'd agreed. That night, she was surprised when a bright pink shirt approached her from a distance. She had thought him conservative, and couldn't remove her gaze from this remodelled Adrian. It was as if she was seeing him for the first time. There was something irregular about Adrian's features. He wasn't a conventionally handsome man but when he smiled a warmth and strength radiated from him. It was his eyes that really connected to her. They pierced her being and made her feel uncomfortable and at ease at the same time.

That ease was disturbed when Precious heard nagging village voices shake her brain, 'This is not allowed¬¬—stick to your kind.' She addressed herself sternly as if chastising another person. 'You've never looked at a man in that way before. Don't for one minute imagine this intelligent Englishman will think of you as anything other than an object of pity or as 'do-gooder' or 'a busy body', as Sergeant Jones likes to call me.'

Adrian was feeling pretty good. He congratulated himself on his choice of pink shirt. Their clothing blended well, he thought, as he admired Precious resplendent in her peacock coloured turban, which complemented the Kenyan printed dress of turquoise and gold. The large circular earrings emphasised her swan-like neck and large dark eyes.

DJ Euton was laid back but confident and charismatic. The welcoming atmosphere made Adrian feel relaxed as he headed for the bar. He jumped as he felt a male hand on his shoulder, turned and smiled in recognition.

'Hey man, what you doing here?' said the owner of the hand.

Adrian introduced Precious saying,

'Jaysee and I go back a long way–to primary school.'

He turned to his old school friend.

'There was something unforgettable about those summer days when my Mum gave us a packed lunch and we'd take our bikes to Hyde Park. You remember how George went with us as far as Kensington Gardens and left us at the Peter Pan Park.' He grinned at Jayzee and the bandana around his head and said, 'It looks like Jaysee has carried on playing pirates.'

'Where you from in Africa?' asked Jaysee.

When Precious said 'Kenya' he looked almost disappointed.

Adrian explained, 'He hoped you were from the other side of Africa. Jaysee's Aunt Dolores took us to watch some guys from Gambia perform, it changed his life.'

'Yea that day is etched into my brain man. They talked all groovy. They talked in a rhythm like the tapping of a woodpecker or a preacher man repeating himself. It was griot, man. It was rap before we knew the word.'

'Youthful rebellion was in the air but I liked what Jaysee started to perform better than the Reggae George and Delroy played all the time.'

Then Adrian shook his head at his friend in mock disapproval.

'You told me that we could rap about anything.' Looking at Precious, he said, 'Jaysee said that he'd teach me but he never did.'

Jaysee gave Adrian a high five and suggested that Precious dance with Adrian and then she'd know why.

'He'd got no rhythm but maybe that's all changed? You look like you can move, lady.'

Adrian felt he had no choice but to ask Precious to dance. She had rhythm and style. Adrian knew the moves but was awkward and reserved. He didn't often feel too white, but on the dance floor he knew he was. Despite that, Precious saw that he enjoyed himself and said as much as he walked her home.

"How about you come to lunch on Sunday next week, and afterwards I'll give you some dancing lessons?' The glimmer of flirtation disappeared almost as soon as it had flickered into life.

'Please don't be offended and take no notice of that Jaysee. I enjoyed our dances but we could make a better go of it if we practiced.'

He wasn't offended. He kissed her goodnight. As she closed the door, she turned and leaned back against it, her eyes half shut in pleasure. This felt dangerous. Did she know what she was doing? And she decided she didn't.

Someone else had seen that furtive kiss.

Precious's colleagues in the police force knew nothing of her private life. There had been no trouble keeping this separation because she didn't really have a private life. The next day, she was surprised and embarrassed when Sergeant Jones commented on a certain white male companion when she passed him at reception. Only he didn't put it quite like that. He put his fingers to his lips and made a crude gesture. For a moment she lost her poise, but she mastered herself and said in a dignified voice,

'Keep your investigations to resolving crimes, Sergeant Jones.'

∞

Precious looked out of the window of her flat to see Adrian staring at the list of names over the buzzers. She opened the window and called down.

'First floor.'

After a lunch of rice, chicken curry and salad, she played a tango saying, 'This isn't exactly disco but it's a good way to match our rhythm.'

They looked good together, being of similar height and build. Adrian made all the right steps but she couldn't help but think he lacked style.

'Think of the way animals move. Sinuous snakes, graceful swans, lion's silently on tiptoe as they stalk their prey. How about for this next number we swing each other around like monkeys going from tree to tree?'

Adrian laughed and acted the part. As they practised he sensed a pulsating in his limbs as if a profound and natural force was taking control of his body. His confidence grew, and when they jived, he threw himself energetically into the dance, enjoying making her move.

But there was more. Precious experienced a deep sensation she had not felt before.

Realising she had been lost in her thoughts for ages, she said,

'We need a drink after all that exercise.'

'I've got to get out of this wet shirt,' Adrian announced. 'I've a T-shirt underneath so I'm quite respectable,' he said as he unbuttoned it.

Precious watched like an African child encountering white men in shorts for the first time as her gaze fixed on his hairy Caucasian body. She hadn't seen Adrian's naked arms before. Instinct set in as she curiously stroked the hairs on his forearm, and when Adrian pulled her close, a current of attraction melded them together like a perfect black and white Yin and Yang.

'Shall we?' he asked. 'Do you feel like I do?'

'Oh yes' she replied. 'Yes, but there's something you need to know.'

A look of anxiety spread across his face.

'It's not what you think' she said. 'In England you rarely come across twenty-eight coming on twenty nine-year old virgins. But that's me. Do you mind?'

Adrian looked astonished. Would he, could he understand her?

'Do you want to tell me about it?'

'As the chief's daughter I was expected to be a virgin when I married.'

'But you have been here for years,' said Adrian.

'The indoctrination went deep. I was taught that my value disappears if I lose my virginity. After that a woman's only worth is as a wife and mother.'

Adrian raised an eyebrow.

'Sure it's nonsense but… I told you how I ran away at sixteen to get a taste of freedom but I'm not free even now. Years of watching my mother suffer as a chief's wife and the humiliation from my step-mother put me off marriage. The job at the women's refuge didn't help either. Lack of trust got in the way of desire.

'I had to work and do my Master's degree at the same time. I hardly had time to sleep, let alone date. It was only a couple of years ago that I allowed myself any personal life and that got swallowed up by Crossroads. You're the first man I've felt this way about. I sense that I can trust you not to take away my independence.'

Adrian squeezed his lower lip and narrowed his eyes as he concentrated hard. The silence seemed heavy but then he smiled and whispered.

'Let's take it slowly. Any time you feel uncomfortable just say 'No' and I'll stop.'

Precious allowed him to undress her in no rush but with a touch heavy with desire and then he gently caressed her breasts. When he'd explored every part of her, he invited her to do the same for him.

That night she slept like a baby, and when she woke, she was surprised to see Adrian staring at her like a bear sated on honey.

Chapter 7: Threats
Plans for Abeo's funeral

Just knowing Adrian was in the world, and knowing he felt about her the way she felt about him, hit her with a shiver of joy. The night she lost her virginity was indelibly imprinted on her mind. It wasn't a visual memory, it was a sensation. Her legs were on fire, her ears resounded like an Indonesian Gamalan and she felt as if she had stopped breathing.

Her pleasure was quickly overshadowed by a call from Abeo's parents. They asked for a meeting with Crossroads trustees to discuss a memorial service. Adrian was invited to come too. He had gained their trust. It was on the understanding that he would report only what was agreed at the end of the meeting.

Joshua Amah stood up and addressed the tense gathering.

'Thank you for coming at such short notice. We didn't want news of our plans to slip out and be revealed by the media.' He looked at Adrian and continued. 'Everyone here is our friend. Outside this room this isn't the case—the murder of our son Abeo is testimony to the contrary. We brought him here at great sacrifice to ourselves in the hope that he would have a better life. We intend to return to Ghana and do not wish to go without our son. This no longer feels like his home. We have arranged for a memorial service next week for Abeo where those who loved him can remember him. We would be grateful for your presence.'

A frisson of sorrow rippled around the table. Precious was moved by Joshua's dignity.

Councillor Abbas replied. 'We understand your decision and appreciate you telling us about it first. It goes without saying that we will do everything we can to help you with the memorial service. Let us know what you want and how you would like us to assist you.

The Memorial Service

The Amahs had chosen the Pentecostal Church, which they attended most Sundays. The building was a large warehouse on an industrial estate and so did not look 'spiritual'. Once inside it felt like a place of worship but less formal than an Anglican or Catholic Church. There were no pews, no stained glass and no altar but the chairs looked towards a small table on which stood a simple wooden cross. The seats for the choir were upholstered in red velvet Precious arrived early with Darrel because she had been asked to give one of the eulogies. When it started to fill up the atmosphere changed. Most of the West Africans came in a group and were wearing a combination of black and red. Precious felt decidedly under-dressed in her shapeless black jacket as she admired the dramatic turbans, the well fitted suits and dresses and bright red beads.

The pastor processed in followed by the Gospel Choir. The sound was large and beautiful and the rhythms reverberated making Precious feel like dancing. The congregation stood up and swayed to the music, echoing the chorus. Most of the white people in the room were not sure what to do. After a few minutes had passed they relaxed and joined in. Once the choir arrived in front of the congregation, everyone sat down and the pastor began.

∞

The weekend after the memorial service Crossroads held a day-long conference to discuss the rising incidents of knife crime and the death of Abeo. They asked Darrel, Precious and Adrian to speak.

As she headed for the community centre, Precious's thoughts wandered from the serious topics to be discussed at the meeting. She chided herself at her trivial concerns but couldn't rid herself of the dilemma. How would she look Adrian in the eye? She didn't want to blush and she didn't want anyone to know about their intimacy—after all, the relationship could be short-lived. Her impression of the relationship between white men and black women was one of an unequal power balance. But then another thought occurred to her—most of the marriages she witnessed in Africa were just as unequal for the woman. That was why she had fled Kenya. She didn't want to be bought or controlled by any man. It would take something extraordinary to make her trust them.

She took a shortcut through a passage that led to the vandalised garden. She had hardly gone twenty yards when she was grabbed from behind. Kicking and struggling Precious fought back. She felt her heel connect with someone's shin but really, it was over before it began. They had considerable fighting experience and she had little. Someone blindfolded her while someone else tied her hands. They dragged her into a garage and pushed her onto a chair.

'We saw that picture in the paper. We know who you are and where you live. Take this as a gentle warning,' a menacing voice said as her arms were pulled back and upwards forcing her head down until the pain was excruciating.

'No interfering Africans in our yard. You better get it. No way.'

They took her outside and pushed her against a wall and she heard their confident steps walking slowly away. Once they had gone, she edged her way along the wall in the direction of the square where they had built the sports area. Someone would soon come along. That someone was Darrel heading for the meeting.

'My god, Precious,' he said as he took off the blindfold and untied her. 'Who did this?'

'I don't know, Darrel. I didn't recognise their voices. Do you think this could be about Abeo?'

'You've got to tell Inspector Ball. They took Nelson in for questioning yesterday.'

Precious rang the inspector but suggested she still attend the meeting.

'Shall we keep things normal, Sir? If I'm not there, people on the estate will suspect something is wrong. As it is, only Darrel knows. Given the rising tension, I think that's the best approach. Is it okay if I come to the station as soon as the meeting is over?'

Inspector Ball agreed. Her attackers would be long gone and there were no witnesses, but he sent two officers to walk the estate.

∞

After the meeting, Adrian approached Precious.

'Can I walk you home?'

'I'm not going home Ade. I—I have to go to the police station.'

'You said you were working regular hours this week. Something has happened, hasn't it?'

'How did you know?'

'Precious you're shaking. Let me get you a taxi.'

While they waited Adrian said in a jokey manner,

'Trust me, I'm a journalist. Whether you do or don't, I've seen enough to know when something traumatic has happened, and its best to get it out—the quicker the better.'

Precious described what had happened.

'It was all over in ten minutes, Ade.'

He looked devastated. 'My feature about you! Christ. It's my fault. I drew their attention to you.'

He suggested he go with her to the station. Without thinking she accepted. It felt good having someone who cared. When she walked into the station with Adrian, she didn't respond to the crude gesture which followed Sergeant Jones's knowing wink of recognition but carried on walking. Some of her colleagues noticed and were about to joke but the sight of the expression of distress on her face silenced them. Her gaze was fixed ahead on the double doors in front of her.

Just as the couple reached them, they swung forwards and Nelson walked into the lobby. He had been released without charge. The arrogant grin on his face sickened Precious as he sauntered out of the station with his lawyer.

Watching him, Precious knew, they all knew, that this would not be the last time Nelson was in trouble with the law. What nobody knew was when.

Chapter 8: Complicated relationships
London 2016: Two months later.

Precious and Adrian saw more and more of each other. Both of them were surprised by the speed at which their relationship was developing.

'I've never wanted to spend so long with anyone before,' Adrian revealed one night in bed. 'I get distracted by my work and don't allow enough time to really get to know a person, but with you...' he trailed off. 'Everything reminds me of you. I find myself bringing you up in conversation, even if it's barely relevant. When I see something funny on the internet, the first thing I want to do is show it to you and make you laugh.' He buried his face in the pillow and let out a groan. 'I sound pathetic.'

'I like pathetic.' said Precious, as she wrapped her arm around his waist and kissed the back of his neck.

He turned to smile into her deep dark eyes and she leant in and kissed him gently.

'I've been thinking...' she said slowly.

'Yes?' he asked, sounding equal parts interested and afraid.

'It doesn't make sense having two flats when we spend all our spare time together anyway. Could it work? It's a step beyond our normal comfort zones but I'm ready to give it a try if you are.'

The silence that met her filled her with cold dread.

'Forget I said it,' she muttered into the silence. 'Don't know what I was—'

'Let's do it,' said Adrian, speaking over her.

'You're sure?' she asked.

'I'm sure,' he smiled, and he moved in to kiss her again.

Precious was surprised by herself. She'd felt so sure that

after her upbringing and her work in the refuge that she'd never trust a man enough to live with him. Somehow, Adrian was different. He listened to her and not in the way which made her think he was waiting for her to finish speaking just so he could move the conversation onto a topic that he wanted to discuss. He offered to do her washing when she left clothes at his house. He didn't insist on paying for everything when they went out, which would have aggravated her. It wasn't like having a relationship with a patriarchal man, but with an equal.

Their friends were taken aback by the change that had taken over their dependably single friends. A glow of happiness was apparent in Precious's smile. Despite that she stayed private and provided monosyllabic answers to any question regarding Adrian and her relationship with him. Adrian took the change more in his stride answering his friends' curious questions. He hoped the contrast was down to their cultural differences and didn't reveal a disparity in enthusiasm.

His theory was partially proved a few weeks after Precious had moved her things into his flat.

'Precious why don't you like facing me when we sleep?'

Precious smiled like a shy child.

'To understand you need to know more about my childhood. When we were growing up my mum took in poor children from the village—mostly the orphans of dead relatives. When I told her that I wished she didn't she scolded me and said, "I cannot see children suffering and not take them in. I do not want to hear you complain again, Precious Lutta."'

'Is that really how your mother talks?' asked Adrian.

'People say I'm a good mimic. It's helped me learn languages.'

'You were telling me about your childhood and you need

58

to answer my question.' prompted Adrian.

'With so many of us, meals were a problem because there were more children in the house than there were plates. The bowl would go around, and you picked your piece of meat and held it close to you in case someone snatched it away. If it was dark when the bowl came around, a naughty child called Mtali would pick more than one piece which meant someone had to go without, and that someone was always me.'

'What has this got to do with you sleeping the other way?' Adrian reminded her.

'It's about the sleeping arrangements for so many children. Kioni separated the boys in one room and the girls in another. She placed a large mat on the floor. The only way to have any cover was to make sure I was in the middle. If the children on both sides pulled the shared cover it meant I stayed covered. But that came at a price. It meant that whichever way I turned I'd have someone's face in my face. Sometimes I'd wake up and it wasn't a face—it was a bottom!

'I'm sorry Adrian but that experience has put me off facing anyone when I sleep. It gives me nightmares. I've come to value my private space so much that it's almost an obsession.'

Adrian chose to change the subject. 'It's time you met my father. I'd rather George didn't turn up and find you.'

'I'd love to meet him, Ade, especially if he's anything like you. We're not a married couple but it still feels like meeting a father-in-law. Tell me about him and what I should call him, please.' The 'please' was spoken with determination.

'You once called me a privileged white man. My father lives in Notting Hill, so you'd expect him to be privileged, but you'd be wrong. George was born in the East End at the end of the war.'

Adrian took out a photo album and showed Precious a snap of a scruffy looking urchin in short trousers with dirty, scarred knees. The four-year-old was standing on top of a dangerous looking pile of debris holding a brass bullet case and looking pleased with himself.

'That was Dad standing on the remains of his grandparents' house. My father's eldest brother and his grandmother were killed in the blast.'

Precious stared hard at the photo. Her preconceptions had changed a lot since 2007 when she'd arrived with stereotypical views of Englishmen. In her work she had observed and listened, in many cases relating to the stories she'd heard.

'Soon after that picture was taken, George's father rented a flat in Notting Hill Gate. It took him a few more years to save for a deposit on a house. The reason Caribbean people of the Windrush generation settled in Notting Hill was because it was cheap and undesirable. Racism meant it was hard finding somewhere to live, and housing was in short supply because of the bomb damage.'

'In my work I heard stories of exploitation by slum landlords like Peter Rackman. Poor housing and homelessness hasn't gone away but it's better than then,' said Precious pointing to the photo.

'Multi-occupation led to multi-problems and then to race riots. According to Dad, the apocryphal notices saying, 'No Blacks, Irish and dogs' were rare. It was more common for those early migrants to turn up to view a flat and be told it was already let. Before they were halfway down the street, they'd watch as the landlady ushered in a white couple. That was the cause of the multi-occupation. But not all whites were unwelcoming. My grandfather got a reputation as an anti-racist activist when Mosley and his racist brown shirts marched through Notting Hill.' Adrian spoke with fierce pride of his father and grandfather, and while it made Precious curious to meet his father she also felt slightly intimidated by how important George was to him.

'Delroy, George's best friend is black—I'll introduce you to him. Dad's well liked in the West Indian community, what's left of it. Renters went a long time ago and some families sold up. Dad inherited the house when grandpa died and we moved in when I was fourteen.'

Chapter 9: August 2016: Meetings
George

It was only after moving in together that Adrian had talked to Precious about his parents. A desperately sad look spread across his face as he said, 'I was thirteen when Mum died. Her death left a gaping hole in George's life. And I suppose in mine too.'

A joy rider had mounted the pavement. His mother had been in the wrong place at the wrong time. He tried his best to explain how painful his father had felt living in the vibrant home Liz had made.

'He felt her presence everywhere. That's why, when my grandfather died, he and I moved into the house in Notting Hill Gate.

'I wasn't keen at the time. I liked the sense of Mum in the house. In Notting Hill I felt eerie echoes of George's childhood. When I was fifteen I started to ask myself, 'Is this what life is all about? Am I destined to repeat my father's life and become a printer?'

Adrian told her how common it was in the world of the closed-shop printing union for sons to follow fathers.

'Every instinct rebelled. A bit like when you felt the need to assert yourself that time you ran away to Uganda. I didn't want a medieval existence where sons took up the same trade as night follows day.

'When I was eleven I was given a tour of the press. I was excited by the buzz of Fleet Street, the tension of demanding deadlines.' As he spoke, Adrian looked as if he was back there.

"It was sheer magnetism, the macho culture throbbing in the rhythmic sound of the press. I watched as the papers emerged as if from a dragon's mouth. After that, the smell of the ink on George's clothes was a constant reminder of what was expected of me. It had its attractions.'

Precious responded by asking him,

'I feel a bit uncomfortable when you call your father George. Why do you call him George and not Dad?'

'Because after Mum died, we were together so much and grew so close, it didn't always feel like father and son. When George talked to me about Mum he called her Liz and not 'mother'. I suppose it is odd, now that you mention it, but it naturally emerged from our relationship.'

∞

The timing was perfect. It was the run up to the Notting Hill Carnival and there was an atmosphere of anticipation as she and Adrian walked down Portobello Road through the antiques market. Precious kept stopping to browse. Artefacts from everywhere in the world was on sale. The stallholders looked as interesting as their goods.

'You're meant to be meeting my dad. We don't want to be late for your first encounter,' said Adrian, trying to get her to focus on moving along.

In Lancaster Road, Precious gazed admiringly at the three-storey terraced house and wondered why Adrian didn't live there. But he did have a key. He opened the door and called to his father. Unlike Adrian's light airy and uncluttered flat, the hallway felt gloomy with its dark red spotted carpet and blocked-in staircase.

George came out from the kitchen, which looked as if it hadn't changed much since he inherited the house. A kippered smell followed him. His hair was thinning on his crown, but it was longer at the neck and tied back in a ponytail. He held out a wrinkled hand to welcome her.

'Come in, come in, 'he said. 'Tea, beer or wine?'

Precious looked uncomfortable. She nodded.

'I think that means tea,' said Adrian.

They sat on the worn but comfortable sofas, looking out at a small overgrown garden.

'It's about time Ade introduced me to a girlfriend. I'd started to think he was copying his old man.'

After tea and polite questions Precious was surprised to see a large black man about the same age as George unlock the door and walk in.

'I see you've got company, George. I can come back later.'

'Delroy, let me introduce you to Precious. This is the first time I've met her too. It's taken Ade long enough. He thought he'd kept it a secret from me but I have my spies. Precious, this is Delroy. We go back a long time. We were best friends at school - well most of the time. Sometimes I had my doubts - he always beat me at football, you see, and that didn't seem fair!'

Delroy noticed some reservation on Precious's part and said, 'Why don't you introduce Precious to the girls next door There was a lot of laughter coming from there as I passed.'

'That's a good idea,' agreed George. 'You'll see at first hand the work that goes into preparing for the Carnival. My neighbour, Dolores, has a team working on costumes.'

'You've met her nephew Jaysee. A warning - if Dolores wants to hug you, protect your ribs!'

The door was unlocked. George opened it and called out as they walked in. Precious felt at home before she was even introduced to anyone. The hilarity and the singing reminded her of Kenya. She sank to the floor took up a needle and a thimbleful of sequins and joined in the sewing. After watching and chatting for a while, George said he needed a fag break. Adrian, Delroy and George left for the pub and said they'd return in an hour.

When they had left, Precious tentatively asked about George and Liz. Had Dolores met her?

Dolores's eyes sparkled with enthusiasm.

'Liz was a force of nature. I liked her from the moment we met when George introduced her to his father. How would I describe her? A daughter of the summer of love—miniskirted and riding a Vespa. No wonder George fell for her at first sight. But life plays cruel tricks. She died just before George inherited the house next door. You noticed that it needs a woman's touch? Sure is a mess. We're all fond of George but we wish he'd met someone else. Shame it is. He's nearly seventy four and set in his ways, isn't he girls? Not so likely that he'll find love again.'

They all nodded and grinned.

Precious's hair was admired. 'Where'd you get it done?'

She smiled, 'It took five hours. If I tell you the name of my hairdresser, promise you'll keep it to yourself. I don't want her getting so busy she can't fit me in.'

Dolores saw Precious glance at a photo of her parents. Delores' mother had tried to straighten her hair to look English and fit in.

'I respect my parents' generation. They arrived with suitcases filled with dreams but had no idea what to expect. The reality was that they felt like strangers in a strange land. But no matter what discrimination and hardship life threw at them they kept their dignity. To the world they smiled through adversity. Once, when my mother thought I wasn't looking, I saw her struggle to hold back the tears.'

A large, loud and jolly lady sang out,

'No more of that Dolores. It's carnival.'

'Try it on, Amantha. Give us a whirl,' said Dolores handing the costume to an eager teenager.

Precious felt accepted and glowed like the rays of sun bouncing off the embroidery into the finished carnival costume. It was like a flash light in her brain. She understood that most of her life had been driven by an impulse to run away in reality or in her imagination. She had made a new life for herself in London but, up until now, it hadn't felt like a home.

'What is 'home'?' she asked herself. 'Is it how I feel today walking with Adrian and experiencing a warm Afro-Caribbean embrace?'

As they walked towards the tube station, Adrian suggested, 'Now that you've met my father, how about you introduce me to yours?'

Panic, doubt and confusion resurfaced.

∞

Precious persuaded Adrian to take her to the Carnival. Dolores and her party of twenty young people of all ages planned to take part in the Sunday family day. They decided to go then rather than on the much busier and noisier Bank Holiday Monday. Adrian suggested they stay overnight on Saturday with George as public transport towards Notting Hill would be sardine-like during the Carnival. They took their places early, ready to watch the parade. Looking at the crowds gathering, Precious said 'I thought you said this is the quieter day, Ade.'

'It is but quiet and Carnival don't agree. Over a million people came last year. But of the two days Sunday is the less crowded.'

'That explains it,' said Precious.

'What did you say?' asked Adrian.

The steel bands and the sound systems were getting louder and louder. That didn't matter. Never in her life had she seen so many colourful outfits. There was something about the style of the dancing that felt African and the costumes were incredible. Then came the Afro beats. She felt at ease. Precious waved enthusiastically as she saw Dolores's float approach them. The children were dressed as peacocks and every kind of tropical and imaginary bird going. Dolores sat like a Queen on her peacock throne at the back of the float under fake palm and banana trees.

'No wonder it takes Dolores so many months to make the costumes.'

Dazzled by the spectacle, Precious hardly noticed the passing of time. Adrian took her by the hand and drew her to a quieter spot, although nowhere could be described as quiet.

'You've experienced the atmosphere and I'm in need of a drink and something to eat. The food's good here but the queues are enormous. Why don't we enjoy the view from above? Let's have a beer on George's balcony.'

∞

'I expect George is with Delroy,' said Adrian, when they realised they were alone in the house. 'You go on upstairs onto the balcony and I'll fetch the beer and sandwiches from the fridge.'

Sat on the third floor overlooking George's garden, Precious could still hear the parade but it was kinder on her ears. Through the gaps between houses she caught glimpses of the floats. Her eye was caught by what looked like a scuffle at a bus stop. She recognised the red bandanas. It didn't surprise her that the Wolf Crew would come to the Carnival: the whole of London appeared to be in the area having a great time.

'Ade, come here, come quickly,' she called. He put down the drinks and looked in the direction she was pointing. He saw the knife but the guy who was targeted leaped into the road and ran towards an approaching steel band and disappeared into the crowd. Precious got on the phone and described what she had seen and where. The Carnival was well policed and in no time at all officers on the scene but the gang had dispersed.

Chapter 10: Disturbing News
September 2016: Kenya beckons

Disturbing dreams returned when Precious received the news that her father had died. He was old. It was expected. It was no tragedy just the natural order of things. But the news churned up feelings of guilt and loss. Her emotions took her by surprise. She had not been to Kenya since she had fled from the arranged marriage. She intended to go back. She frequently spoke of it, and even planned it, pricing out the cost and looking at her holidays. But something always stopped her.

Now she had no choice. Being the chief and an ancestor of the Tanga tribe meant a state funeral where all the tribesmen had to attend dressed in traditional regalia. The extensive customs surrounding death were fuelling her nightmares. She tried explaining it to a bewildered but curious Adrian.

'When a person is dead, they are still considered to be around, at least in their spirits. Weeping and crying out loud is compulsory and expected. People close to the deceased are supposed to weep more than anyone else! It can go as far as crawling on the ground and tearing off clothes. The neighbours help the bereaved family weep uncontrollably and the true test of unity is shown if their grief has moved their neighbours.'

'That sounds like a lot of pressure. I'm sorry Precious. Am I going to be in the way?' asked Adrian. Precious was worried but didn't share her concerns with Adrian. She liked the idea of not going 'home' alone.

'You may even enjoy it because the funeral is followed by a great celebration, the family hosting from dozens to hundreds of people for a period of forty days, many camping out. You'll be swept up in it, Adrian.'

'I wish I could've met your father, but if I come with you, at least I'll meet the rest of your family. I'm owed some holiday and I've never been to Kenya.'

'I'd love that,' said Precious but once alone her thoughts were less positive.

'What will happen to Ade? He has no idea how conservative attitudes are in rural Kenya. If we're together, they'll expect us to be married. We could pretend to be married, but a man cannot attend his father-in-law's funeral until he pays dowry,' she reminded herself and dashed that idea as she fell asleep.

In her dream she saw a grave covered in bananas and woke in a panic. Girls who die in their parents' home before they get married are buried behind the house near the fence or in the banana plantation because they are considered as foreigners who could bring a curse to the family. In her vision it was she who was cursed and driven out.

Adrian woke early but was unaware of how early. He was turning over and over in his mind impressions of Africa. He liked seeing it through David Attenborough's eyes.

'What's it really like? Not all wildebeests running across the savannah or lions chasing giraffes for sure,' he said out loud.

'What time is it?' Precious croaked, looking at her mobile '5.30. It's not worth going to sleep again I have to be up soon. Is something wrong?'

'Not really. It's just that we haven't actually talked about this trip, have we? It's been organised in a rush because of the funeral and we are both full on at work.'

'You're right. What would you like to know?'

Adrian hesitated wondering how to ask Precious tactfully what to expect in a remote rural area?

'Tell me more about your family—more about your father. Was he very proud of your achievements?'

'How would I know?' replied Precious.

'Surely you wrote and told him?'

'Yes, but he never replied. My mother and I used to write to each other every month. She speaks English but can only read simple English. Because she left school at fifteen, she doesn't write it well. She wrote to me in Swahili but nowadays with the internet, my elder sister Nechesa and my half- sister Aluna passes on messages. I told you that my oldest sister Mosi died when I was eight.

'But your father cutting you off like that. Was he still angry with you about leaving? We never really finished that story, did we?'

'I really don't know Adrian and I can't ask him now. I expect it was because I'm guilty of being female, so anything I achieve doesn't really count. But you needn't worry. You'll be given a great welcome.'

Part 2: Kenya

1958 Chief Kidake to Barack Hussein Obama [2] (Sr)

Kioni has given birth to a third daughter. I must take a second wife. I must have a son or the succession will be disputed and that could endanger the safety of my people. Kioni is angry with me. She's been influenced by her father and the missionaries who say a man should only have one wife. We've learned to care for each other, but I am the chief and I need an heir.

The splits in Mau Mau and between the tribes of Kenya could spell disaster. You told me that Independence will come sooner than many people think. I've come to support Jaramogi Oginga Odinga. I like to think he will unite us and do what is best for our country. Independence is on the horizon, but who knows what will happen when the British leave and under what circumstances they will depart.

---

2 The father of President Barack Obama

Chapter 1: Stories and untold stories
Heathrow October 2016

They sipped Kenyan tea from disposable cups as they waited for their flight to Nairobi. The ebullient Precious was unusually quiet. Adrian broke the silence.

'Precious I want you to give me ten reasons why I should want to go to Kenya.'

'Elephants, lions, zebras, antelope, cheetahs, giraffes, rhinos, leopards, flamingos, buffalos and baboons. That's eleven.'

'You can do better than that. That much I can do myself. I need you to tell me about the people and the culture but situate them in the landscape. Location and climate are part of who we are, unless you live in a darkened room constantly looking at a screen.'

'Nairobi, safaris and the coast are a world away from village life, Ade. Are you sure you want to come with me to the funeral? I'll understand if you want to use your holiday to enjoy Kenyan tourism.'

'But it's because of you that I'm going to Kenya. I want to see where you come from.'

Precious was struggling to know how to introduce Adrian to her village—something she'd never imagined would happen. She wondered how everyone was going to receive him? How would she feel walking around with him in the muddy village? She had to prepare him.

'I'm sorry, Ade, I've been less than communicative. You must think it's because of the funeral. It's not. It's about how to tell you what to expect, how to behave. I don't think you'll like it. '

'Try me,' said Adrian.

Flight Number KQ101 to Nairobi is now boarding.

∞

Half an hour into the journey Adrian tried again.

'Do you remember when we met? I suggested you start at the beginning and tell me about your childhood? You told me about your desire to leave but not what happened to make you leave.'

Precious didn't want to revisit that conversation; it felt as turbulent as a plane flying through storm clouds. Something in her didn't want Adrian to go to the village. How could she put him off?

'Why am I sitting next to a journalist? All these probing questions! I'll tell you a story but then you must tell me more about your childhood too.

'Once upon a time in a faraway village,' Adrian grinned as Precious began. 'there lived a little girl. It was customary for an animal to be slaughtered for special occasions, and once it was slaughtered it was the custom to share the meat. The people in the village would carefully carve the pieces and wrap them in banana leaves, and the children would be asked to take them to the other families.

'This particular day it was the little girl's turn to take the goat's meat to another homestead. She dawdled and darkness fell. She was terrified, as she had heard rumours of a leopard being spotted. Metallic sounds rattled in her head and her mind started to play tricks on her. She remembered a few weeks earlier she had woken to hear her mother drumming tins and pots, trying to scare the leopard away and stop it from breaking into the hut where the animals were kept for the night. When the girl asked her mother why she didn't run away from the leopard, she said "I've had enough of our sheep being eaten by the same leopard. We must chase it away with the machete or run". But this time, the little girl was all alone without a machete.'

'So, did you chase it away?' asked Adrian.

'My mother taught me how to react – make lots of noise– so I clapped my hands and walked steady and fast. I didn't run. Instead I made loud trilling sounds and felt so grown up when I arrived safely.'

Precious looked at Adrian. 'Now it's your turn.'

'I haven't got anything to match that. The scariest animals at my school in Kilburn were human.'

'Okay,' said Precious, keen for the attention to be diverted away from her. 'Then tell me a story about your dad.'

'I was ten years old when Rupert Murdoch moved his newspapers out of Fleet Street to Wapping. This was before he founded Sky, so they were what mattered to him in 1986. This was when unions were losing their power. Not long before that Mum and her friends fundraised for the striking miners and sent food to Wales. I don't think the world is a better place for workers having less clout but the print unions were nepotistic. I told you how George assumed I would follow him and become a print worker – these were well-paid jobs and were mostly inherited. They had a name: 'closed shop'.'

Precious interrupted.

'It sounds like a working class version of the Royal Family. They're expected to join the family firm whether they like it or not. I wonder what my step brother is thinking? Nechesa says he's a professor in the States but they'll assume he'll come back and take on the role of chief.'

'That working class nepotism is long gone thanks to Rupert Murdoch's drive to modernise. He dismissed the thousands who'd downed tools, and brought in members of a maverick electrician's union to keep the printing presses running, said Adrian

'I remember the anxiety on the day when George didn't come back from the picket line. The police were accused of being heavy-handed and aggressive in dealing with strikers and local residents. They made over a thousand arrests, and dad was one of them. It was as if the world I had grown up in had broken. The police let him go the next day, but George was out of a job. Maybe your brother-in-law will be a Murdoch and upset the status quo?'

'I haven't seen Osundwa since I was a teenager. Last time he came to the village I was away at university. I don't feel that I know him. I'm sorry to disappoint you Adrian.'

Precious didn't give him a chance to reply but instead asked,

'How did you manage when George was out of work?'

'My mum worked full time in a boutique. She loved it, but it didn't pay well. She understood better than George how computers were going to change the world of work. The previous Christmas she had saved hard to buy me a second hand Commodore 64. She knew that I wouldn't be following him.'

'Mmm, that's interesting. Most people today are unwilling to acknowledge how Artificial Intelligence will affect employment, just like your father didn't see it coming. Your mother sounds like she was ahead of the curve.'

Adrian smiled sadly and nodded.

'Where we're going mobile phones are changing lives for the better, but it will feel like something from the past to you, Adrian.'

Precious knew she needed to prepare him, even if it would be a difficult conversation. There was so much he didn't know about Kenya, so much he wouldn't understand. She had to get him to agree that there would be no touching in public, no holding of hands or even walking together. However hard Adrian would find it to understand, she had to tell him before they landed in Kenya.

The stewardess delivered their plastic wrapped meal and

they sat together in a comfortable silence. Adrian read a book and Precious looked out the window, wondering why she couldn't bring herself to tell him what he needed to know.

Chapter 2: The problem with being a girl.
Nairobi

The tyres of the Dreamliner squealed as they hit the tarmac at Jomo Kenyatta International Airport. Precious felt nervous. Her mind was racing with worry after worry. She tried to drive out the nagging thoughts but with no success.

'Will I be welcomed back? Will anyone from the family meet me at the airport? What about Adrian, will he be accepted? What if he isn't? What will I do? I never reconciled with Dad, but I still love him. How will that make me feel at the funeral?'

She glanced towards Adrian who was peering round her out the window. The view was much the same as any other airport, big square buildings flanked by white planes glaring in the sun. As the seatbelt signs went off the Kenyan Airways theme tune kicked in and they were welcomed to Nairobi.

Precious helped Adrian fill in a visa and immigration form and, after paying over $50 and waiting in a long queue to have his passport stamped, they headed out of the airport. Precious's fears vanished when she saw Aluna waving vigorously. Aluna, whose company she enjoyed, was Precious's younger half-sister, the only daughter of Mama Murono. Aluna had looked up to Precious throughout their childhood, and sometimes her desire for Precious's attention had made her conjure up elaborate, and often unsuccessful, practical jokes. When Precious thought back on her time in Kenya, her memories of Aluna were not of the annoyance she'd felt at the time, but of the fun and laughter.

Once outside, a large group of men hassled them, each promising them the best deal on a taxi. They hurried passed them; Aluna had a car waiting for them. She was the same cheerful, mischievous person that Precious remembered.

She laughed freely and lost no time giving them all the gossip, who'd married or eloped with whom and who'd died since Precious had last been in touch. She was warm and kind to Adrian.

She spoke English but preferred her native tongue. Ten minutes into the journey, she engaged Precious in an inordinately long conversation in Luhyia and Adrian felt left out. His awkward body language was so obvious that it prompted Precious to do some translating.

'A good start!' Precious thought ironically.

At the hotel, Adrian headed for the loo and Precious took the opportunity to ask her cousin one her biggest worries, 'How will Mama Kioni take to Adrian?'

'To be honest, Precious, I don't know.' She paused, sighing. 'You know how Ma can be. You coming home and dad's funeral… it's a lot to take in without worrying about your relationship with Adrian. Try not to fret. Take Adrian around Nairobi first, before you depart for the village. I promised to leave this evening, but I'll see you in Tusanda.'

∞

Tired after the eight-hour flight, they felt in need of a good wash and rest. Refreshed, Precious resolved that she would tell Adrian her concerns about walking through town with him and visiting the village. But when he walked out of the bathroom, the look of happy contentment dissolved her conviction.

'I'll tell him in the morning,' she promised herself as they fell asleep.

∞

The next day, as they prepared to leave the hotel, she broached the subject. If she didn't tell him now, it would be too late.

'Adrian, I may not have mentioned this, but growing up I

was taught that black girls walking around with white men, especially white men slightly older than them, are prostitutes. I know that's not true for us, but would you mind if, maybe, we could act slightly differently in public?'

'What do you mean?'

'Well, I think it would be best if we don't hold hands. In fact, it's probably best if we're not seen together at all. You can just walk a few steps behind. I know it's not ideal, but it's just while we're here.'

'But in the village we can go on being a normal couple?'

'Well, no. I was going to ask, if you wouldn't mind, if I can introduce you as a newsman who's come to report on a chief's funeral?'

A look crossed Adrian's face—a look she had never seen before. Panicked, Precious continued talking faster and more loudly.

'Sorry, I can't bear being judged. You know I'm not a prostitute, and if people see us holding hands or even walking next to each other, that's what they'll think.'

'Why do you worry about what people think? If you feel ashamed to be seen with me, should I go back to England? I don't want to embarrass you or cause you any problems with your family. Why didn't you tell me this before we left? If I'd known I wouldn't have come.'

'No, don't go, Adrian. I'm so sorry I didn't tell you before. I kept trying but I knew you'd be upset and I didn't want to ruin the trip. There's so much I have to tell you, like how I got to England, but every time I try and tell you I feel so sad and upset. I tried to talk about it on the plane but somehow...' Precious started to cry.

'Okay, let's get out of here and have a coffee, and then you can tell me your story. You go first and I'll join you in the café you choose.' Precious felt a rush of gratitude as Adrian pulled her into a hug. She could feel the tension in his body and knew that he was still annoyed, but at least he seemed to understand.

Bizarrely, on his first full day in Kenya, Adrian found himself in a separate taxi for the hour's drive into the heart of Nairobi. Up ahead, Adrian saw acres and acres of earth painted orange. He leant forward and asked the taxi driver what it was.

'That is Kibera, the slums of Nairobi.'

Adrian tried to focus and as they drew closer. He saw that the orange earth was thousands of rusting corrugated iron roofs. They passed a high rise under construction. In his mirror, the taxi driver saw Adrian's curious gaze and guessed his thoughts.

'The government is knocking down slum dwellings and building new apartments for those people. The flats command a high rental value, being so close to the city centre, so the slum dwellers allocated the accommodation let their flats to make money and move their family elsewhere. Welcome to Nairobi,' he added bitterly.

Adrian's attention moved to huge piles of rubbish beside the road. He saw two small children, neither more than five years old, rummaging through the waste. He watched in horror as one of them picked up something and put it in his mouth. He'd expected to see poverty, but this was beyond anything he had ever imagined.

The taxi came to a stop in the gleaming, ordered first world of central Nairobi. Adrian slid out the cab and entered the coffee house. A subdued Precious waved to him, and he sat down opposite her. Once their coffee and cake arrived, she hesitantly began to try and explain her behaviour, her confidence growing as she saw that Adrian wasn't going to get angry again. After what he'd just seen, he felt like he was prepared for anything.

'When I finished university, my father and uncles decided

it was time to marry me off to the highest bidder. I was valuable property because of my education. A man called Omollo was prepared to pay the most dowry but he was twenty years older than me. I remember the first time I saw him, he was sweating so much in the sun and the smell was horrendous. His face was ugly and squashed and the thought of his… him inside me made me feel physically sick.' Precious paused and took a deep breath.

'Worse still was that I was seen as a commodity – a way for my family to make money. That time I ran away to Uganda for a day when I was fourteen I was striking out not as a girl but as an individual. If I hadn't made that journey alone as a teenager, I'm not sure we'd ever have met, Ade. When I saw those old men discussing my bride price with my father, I was shaken to the core, almost paralysed by revulsion. Then I remembered how easy it had been to go to Uganda as a fourteen-year-old.

'Running away from that marriage was different, because it meant that I couldn't return. Now my father is dead, I have to return but I don't know what kind of reception we'll get. I should have told you before. There was no way I could allow those men to determine my future just as they had determined my mother's life.

'It was trauma that instilled in me this desire to run away which I have to struggle with all the time if I am to achieve anything. I find it hard to settle anywhere. Even in London, where I feel more at home, the itch hasn't completely gone away. I was wrong not to tell you this before. I didn't lie to you. I came to do a Masters and I stayed. But I wanted to put the past behind me.'

'What did you do when you got to Uganda, did you stay with Nechesa?'

'Yes, she took me in, once again. She's always looked after me.

'Will I meet Nechesa?' asked Adrian.

'Yes, she'll be at the funeral and will just love talking to you. You'll like her husband, Otieno, too. He's Ugandan but spoke Luhyia like us. Nechesa likes to boast a lot including repeating that she was taught the Queen's English but once you get to know her you'll like her.

'I told you about the time I ran away when I was sixteen. I stayed overnight with her and Otieno and their first child Rose who was two and a half. Nechesa was teaching full time so needed a house helper. That servant was only eleven. I remember her mother bringing little Risper to start work the afternoon I arrived. It was her first job and I wondered how she would be able to look after Rose when she was just a child herself? I shared the only spare room in the house with her. She slept on the floor in the foetal position and wet the bed that night.

'It made me terribly sad. I lectured Nechesa, pointed at Risper and said, "She should be at school." I berated her until she felt like throwing me out. She rang home soon after I arrived knowing our mother would be worried, so I wasn't surprised when she put me on the bus that afternoon.

'When I fled the second time, I felt like my family had used me, just like Risper's. We only mattered to them because of the money we could make them.'

Adrian's anger diminished as his empathy and imagination allowed him to entered Precious's world.

'Let's go for a walk, somewhere we can walk side by side and you can tell me more. We never properly finished that interview, did we? Remember—the first time we met?'

As they walked out of the café, Precious looked more relaxed. She took in the other customers. There was a woman in a hijab – she was probably from Somalia– talking to a woman of Indian ancestry in a sari. There were faces of every colour as well as black. This was not how she remembered

Nairobi. She spotted a mixed-race couple. It felt different to how she remembered it – a bit more like London.

Precious led them to Nairobi Uhuru Park, a popular destination adjacent to the central business district of Nairobi.

Sounding more her enthusiastic London self, she explained, 'The park was opened by the first president of Kenya, Mzee Jomo Kenyatta. It's called Uhuru which means freedom. Look over there—that lake is artificial.'

'I like it,' said Adrian. 'It reminds me a bit of Hyde Park. It's got a buzz about it.'

She smiled.

'And they're both famous destinations for political activism. A protest was led by my hero, Wangari Maathai. She was the first African woman to win the Nobel Peace Prize because of her tree planting campaigns. What I love about her projects is how they empower and connect ordinary people despite tribal differences. In this city, they love her because she opposed the construction of a sixty-storey business complex which would have destroyed this park.

'You know Ade, when I was threatened after Abeo was murdered, I said over and over again to myself "Remember Maathai – remember her courage." She was beaten and went into hiding for a while. Her supporters were worried that if she was arrested an 'accident' would happen while in custody.'

Precious headed for a particular spot. For the first time since they arrived in Kenya she smiled directed at Adrian and laughed as she said,

'This is the spot where in1996, a Catholic cardinal and an Archbishop burned a heap of condoms. I hope you don't copy them.'

Soon they were walking side by side.

'So,' Adrian prompted, 'we were with the sixteen-year-old you looking at Risper and drawing parallels with your own life.'

'Yes, but I realised that the big difference was my mother. She'd never give me away as a household help. I expect I've already mentioned how proud she is, despite the repeated attempts to humiliate her. When she felt oppressed by Mama Murono, she held her head high and said to me, "I am Kioni, the daughter of Ndula, the man who brought Christianity to my village. My father was so proud of me, his first daughter, that he took me to Butere to the first school for girls run by nuns. They spoke the Queen's English. That's why I am married to the chief because I was the perfect wife." That's who Nechesa gets it from! ' laughed Precious.

Adrian grinned because Precious was obviously trying to imitate her mother's voice and he had heard it before. Her sister was not the only person in the family to sometimes repeat things.

'All her life, Mum regretted being taken out of school early to marry my father. That's why she was so adamant that even though we were girls, we should get a proper education. But she had to fight for it. When my father refused to pay my school fees she worked so hard to earn the money. She grew vegetables and sold them at the market. When she asked me to accompany her to the market it was the highlight of my week. I'd rush back from school ready to walk the six kilometres to Sumo. The pride of being picked to go with her was so exciting I didn't care how far I had to walk.

'Once nearly everything was sold, Mum sent me to buy the family supplies like sugar or salt. If there was any spare cash, I was allowed to go to the little kiosk at the corner of the market that sold the only delicacy available—pieces of meat and ugali, a local staple bread. It was worth the effort because, I sometimes went hungry.'

Adrian empathised. 'After my Mum died, I did a lot of the shopping. No online ordering then, but I enjoyed it. Like you, I was a familiar face in the market, but the big difference between us was that I didn't have to walk miles.'

'You're right, the distance was the real difficulty. On a lucky day we made sales quickly, but at other times it took so long to sell the last remaining vegetables, it was dark before we left the market for the long walk home. It wasn't like walking down Portobello Road!

'Mum often said, "Beware wild animals and witchcraft. Pick three big stones and put one on your head and one in your right hand and one in the left. If you see someone suspicious or an animal and feel threatened use the stone in your right hand, then the one in your left hand. If the person or animal doesn't run use the one on your head. If nothing moves - RUN!"' Precious smiled affectionately at the memory of her mother's words.

'If she hadn't worked so hard, we would never have met, Ade. She scrimped and saved to pay for my education. Look how I paid her back, leaving her to take the blame for my desertion.'

Adrian could hear the guilt and shame in her voice. They walked in silence and he let the park wash away some of the despair before he spoke again and tried to change the subject.

'I like your animal stories. Let's face it, when most Brits think of Africa that's what they see in their minds.'

Precious took advantage of the opportunity to change the subject from her struggles.

'One night as we were walking back, my mother stopped and whispered in a tiny voice, "See those two bright torches? They are the red eyes of a leopard. They gleam in the dark. Stay still until it passes." I stopped breathing. I was so scared I could have died. She assured me that leopards don't bother humans unless you threaten them. She was right; the leopard moved majestically across the road as if it didn't know we were there. How did she know just from the eyes? My mother was my hero. I knew that when I grew up, I wanted to be like my mother—not afraid of anything. When I heard about Maathai I knew that women can change the world.'

'Tell me more about how your mother paid for your education,' suggested Adrian, keen to distract Precious out of the sadness and guilt that kept reappearing in her expression.

'She kept chickens and supplied the local school with eggs. When the demand was too high and she couldn't meet it, she formed a women's cooperative to keep enough poultry to meet the demand.

'Kioni urged the women to use the income to educate their girls. She believed in girl's education but not my father! He contributed nothing. Parents only invest in boys' education. Educating a girl is considered educating someone's wife, and why would you do that? The only reason you'd spend money educating a girl is if they thought it would increase her bride price.'

'I want to meet Kioni. The real question, the really big question is do you want me to meet her?'

'I'm sorry, Ade. I wish we were going to Tusanda to meet my mother and not to bury my father. I'm worried about how my uncles will treat me. That's why I've been so stupid. The only good thing about it is –you will meet EVERYONE and I mean everyone –this will be big.'

'We should have talked more before we left. We don't find enough time to talk, do we? Not surprising really, given our careers and different schedules. I don't know how to say this Precious. I care about you.'

'I know you do but we're not married and that could be awkward in Tusanda. I should have told you in London before we left. I should probably have come on my own, but it felt like having a warm coat on a freezing cold day knowing you were coming with me.

'They won't believe that you'd ever marry me. They'll

categorise me as a prostitute. I know that I shouldn't care but I do. My pride has hurt you, Ade, and come between us but I don't want to hurt my mother either.'

Adrian looked uncomfortable, but he turned and took a long, deep look at Precious. He took in her dark, calm eyes and her beautiful arching brows. At last he understood, and his expression changed to one of love and pride.

Precious gave him a thankful smile. Her ebony skin shone like polished gold.

'This isn't the right moment. I see that. But when we get home maybe we can think about getting married? My old man would say I've left it far too long. What do you say to that?'

Precious said nothing but her silence was radiant.

Chapter 3: First Impressions
Tusanda

Early the following morning they boarded a much smaller aircraft than the one that had brought them to Kenya, and set off for Kisumu. From the air, the landscape varied from a dense city to miles of open arid land. In the distance there were dramatic natural rock formations and the towering outline of Mount Kenya.

Adrian looked out of the window as the plane approached Kisumu and the reflection in Adrian's gaze was vivid green. Were those rice fields? As the plane banked the vast Lake Victoria came into view. Much of the lake was covered in dense vegetation.

Precious guessed his thoughts.

'It may look beautiful but that's Water Hyacinth. It's a menace because it blocks out light and causes the water to stagnate. Those little dots are fishing boats, but they are nor powerful enough to fight their way through it. At times when the entire lake is covered the fishermen have no income. Even though it looks like paradise, life here can be tough.'

Adrian had expected something much smaller and rougher than the sophisticated airport at Kisumu. Precious explained excitedly that Barack Obama's grandmother lived not far away and everybody said that was the reason for such an investment.

'Welcome to Africa!' she said with a grin that Adrian had worried she'd left behind in London.

Walking down the steps of the plane Adrian was struck by the difference in temperature. He'd found Nairobi not too different to London, but this was hot. There was no customs, so they were out swiftly, and were once again accosted by desperate taxi drivers. Precious steered them through to a waiting vehicle. It belonged to Frank, a family friend who lived in Sumo, the nearest town to Tusanda. He was charming and spoke good English, so there was no need for Precious to translate.

Kisumu was bustling. Adrian's eyes fixed on the motorbikes some with five people on them. Some transported huge sofas, some carried building materials and others had three metre tubes strapped sideways so that they were wider than the biggest lorries. Adrian couldn't see a single person wearing a crash helmet! Frank saw the look of amazement on his face.

'A friend of mine accidentally drove over a set of trailing rods from a motorcycle. His bike did a somersault. The riders were not seriously injured but they were lucky.'

They arrived at a tin shack by the lake edge. Adrian thought that to describe it as 'basic' was an understatement but it was clean. The café's menu consisted of one dish Tilapia, a type of fish you could eat dry or wet, with ugali or chips and local vegetables. Precious urged Adrian to try ugali made from maize flour. After stopping at the equator for the obligatory photo, they headed onwards to the Chief's homestead and Precious's ancestral home. For the first time, Adrian was seeing the rural Kenya of Precious's memory—a constant stream of people passing shacks or kiosks containing small businesses. In the fields, women worked while the men sat and chatted. On they went through five police checkpoints, weaving around planks with nails driven through point side up to prevent anyone dodging across. Checks were done on their driving licences, insurance, first aid kit and fire extinguisher.

'Any failures means an on the spot payment to the officer,' Precious explained after the first checkpoint. 'If you can't pay, a trip to the court and an overnight stay in police custody is the consequence, so people prefer the fine. The police here are paid little and this is how they top up their earnings.

But some really corrupt officers have accumulated sufficient wealth to own several properties, which they rent out to earn even more money.'

The police were curious about the muzungu passenger and wondered what this white person was doing. After the first stop Precious grinned.

'With a muzungu as a passenger our drive will be easy. *Muzungu* is Kiswahili for a white man, Ade.'

Precious was right; the police were friendly at every stop and let them pass unhindered. After almost two hours they approached Tusanda. The road was red dust, in contrast to the verdant green of the vegetation.

'I wasn't expecting to see so much green.' Adrian said, turning to Precious.

'And this is the dry season. Those are fields of sugar cane and those over there are maize.' She pointed to the tall green plants lining the fields.

Adrian noticed that there were paths leading through the crops to clusters of mud huts. Some had grass roofs and others were made of corrugated tin.

Everywhere he looked his eyes were drawn to people going about their lives. Tall, elegant women walked straight-backed, carrying ten-litre bottles of water on their heads without spilling a drop. Adrian wondered how they could take the strain and walk with such grace over the uneven ground.

As the car left the smooth tarmac and headed down the bumpy road on the last bit of their journey, Adrian couldn't believe the dust that engulfed the car as Precious shouted, 'Close the windows.'

The car turned up a wide path bordered by trees. Adrian had his first glance of the family home in the distance. The compound was beautifully kept with neatly clipped grass, a hedge full of bougainvillea blossoming in the brilliant sunshine and large shady trees, some with bright red flowers and others a seductive blue. Birds of exotic colours flitted between the trees and from somewhere in the distance came the soothing sound of a charadridae. Adrian smiled at Precious. He wanted to kiss her but controlled himself with great effort.

'You've brought me to Eden!' he said.

Adrian spotted the change on Precious's face. He reached out for her hand.

'Are you okay, darling?'

'I will be once we get through the reception, whatever it will be'.

As they approached the bamboo wooden gate, they were spotted by Nyarotsho, an old neighbour. She started to wail, *'Eee; mama ooo: omwana waliyakora; lelo achelele;'* (My goodness, the lost child has come back)

Precious sobbed silently.

They spotted some children running after the vehicle. When they came to a stop, more and more people came out of the huts, some holding each other and crying noisily. Precious could not see her mother among the crowds. Aunt Nanjira stood in the entrance of the main house and raised both hands to stop everyone from wailing and said,

'Please; please let the guests get in so we can pray for journey mercies before we overwhelm them.'

She was like the respected conductor of an orchestra. The noise and the jostling stopped.

'Where's Mum?' Precious asked.

'Welcome my niece. She is inside waiting for you.'

As was tradition Kioni was sat next to the coffin on the right under a big portrait of her father in his full colonial chiefs' uniform above the coffin. Aunty Najiara holding Precious's hand took her to view the body first before she could speak to anyone.

Mama Murono stood up and started singing. When she finished she said

'Let us pray.'

Kioni sat still and watched as if the world had collapsed under her feet and she was dreaming. Then she stood up and took a few steps towards Precious and they fell into each other's arms hugging and sobbing for what felt like hours; *Mwanawanje Omukosi, Mwanawanje Omukosi;* Kioni kept saying; they held each other so close as if they never wanted to let go ever again. This time Kioni was never going to let her youngest child leave her! She had lost the chief and she wasn't going to lose her youngest daughter.

∞

The house was bigger and more modern than Adrian was expecting and certainly different to the other homes he had seen on the way into Tusanda. It was made of brick and had electricity. When Adrian asked for the loo, he was pleased to be shown to an inside bathroom with flushing toilet and a shower. Soon his attention was not on sanitary provisions but the people.

He emerged to see Precious with her mother.

Her mother kept repeating over and over,

'My daughter, my daughter...'

Soon the room was crowded and Adrian had no idea who all the people were who thrust out a hand to greet him.

They were given drinks to take outside. Quite a crowd had gathered. Since Kisumu, he hadn't seen a white face. He wondered if Precious had felt this way when they'd gone to visit friends in Hampshire and hers had been the only black face. He'd been relieved that she hadn't noticed the group of teenagers make jungle noises. At least here, the people staring at him looked not hostile but curious. So far, he had been warmly greeted and welcomed by everyone. He couldn't understand why Precious had flipped in Nairobi.

After a meal, Paul, Precious's cousin, offered to show Adrian around the village while the closest family members attended a meeting. It took what felt like hours to get a short distance. At every home they passed they were invited in. Everyone seemed to know everyone else.

Paul noticed the surprise on his face. 'They just want you to feel welcome.'

'Sorry Paul. I was thinking about how we live in England. I don't even know the names of many of the closest neighbours in my block of flats.'

Adrian thought that the poorest accommodation in the Wentworth estate would feel like luxury to the people he was meeting. The houses were made from mud and he saw not a single water tap.

'How do they get water?' asked Adrian.

'From the river and lighting comes from a kerosene burner or solar light, cooking is on three stones with a wood or charcoal fire and the toilet is a hole in the ground,' said Paul.

'The chief's house is one of the few with modern facilities. The large storage tank in the kitchen holds clean water. It's suppled from a borehole and you noticed that the house has electricity.'

Adrian was barely listening. He felt self-conscious as everyone they passed looked at him. When eventually he was shown to his room and taught how to fasten the mosquito net, he thought he would sleep instantly. Then he heard a noise. There was no distant noise of traffic to drown out the strangely high pitched sound—the loud hum of mosquitoes.

∞

Uncle Moses, her father's youngest brother, was in charge

of the funeral arrangements. He summoned the children to gather in the chief's bedroom. The large round room displayed Chief Kidake's regalia including his three-legged stool, a big colonial looking round hat and a khaki uniform. Precious pictured him wearing it to the chief Baraza meetings. In the most prominent position was a framed picture of the Queen of England. Kidake had been presented with it when he had attended Elizabeth II's coronation.

Only the chief's siblings, children and wives were allowed to enter the private room with the body. Her heart raced. The last time she had seen the man in the coffin was not a time she wanted to remember.

Her mother took her seat on the right-hand side, the first wife's position, and Mama Muruno sat on the left. On either side of them were two women she did not recognise. Then she remembered Nechesa's email explaining that their father had taken two wives from the city after his third wife died five years ago. They were the same age as her and Nechesa!

Precious struggled to control her emotions. The disregard of the interests of women, the sacrifices expected of them made her flinch with anger. She forced herself to look at the casket and felt a physical shock ripple through her. Without the man who lay inside, she would not have been born. All his energy, confidence and life force were gone. Her feeling of sorrow evoked strange thoughts. Did he know they were all there? Did he know that she had returned?

The girls were sat in one corner and the boys in the other. She wondered at the segregation of men and women, even during sad moments like this. Precious recognised just how much she had changed in the time she had been away.

She caught sight of one of her half-brothers. Just seeing Samuel brought back painful memories of the big family tree and how she watched as her father had turned her away, telling her he couldn't pay her school fees because he had just paid Samuel's. 'What's he doing with his life?' Precious wondered. 'Has he done well for himself after that privileged education from the chief?' She looked around for the first-born son, Osundwa, who would succeed her father, but she couldn't see him.

In one corner, Nechesa sobbed quietly.

'Maybe she developed a better relationship with the chief despite helping me escape? He was certainly angry with her when he found out I was with her in Uganda,' she mused to herself.

Uncle Moses banged his stick for quiet.

'I have called you together to remind you of the importance of the rituals you will be part of. Our ancestors expect that tradition is followed.'

He paused, disturbed by a cousin crying, then continued.

'We share the pain of loss but as royals we are not to be seen as weak. We must be strong for the rest of the tribe, especially the men. Remember Chief Kidake was a great leader of his people as was his father, your grandfather Omogo, king of our people. He has left fifteen of his children and four great wives. So, make him proud.' Aluna dried her eyes.

'It is my duty to remind you of the rules. All married daughters must go back to their marital homes to inform your husbands and in-laws of the times and rituals. You must wail as you near the homestead to alert everyone that you are approaching. You must not enter the compound until you are met by the oldest person in the homestead, and once you enter, inform them of the burial day. The ritual of 'taking the dead man's spirit to your home' must be followed. If there is any outstanding dowry, it must be paid before the burial day on Thursday. On that day, the in-laws must attend the funeral with a bull, a bag of maize and ten chickens.'

Precious was anxious about what was going to happen.

Should she tell them about her relationship with Adrian and their intended marriage plans? What will they say? Would they accept him, a white man? As she looked at her uncle, she guessed that he was going to embarrass her. 'Will he remind everyone of my terrible deed?'

He cleared his throat, 'As for you Precious, you know the shame you brought to the family and your father's sadness and humiliation. You must come and meet with me and other clan elders to discuss what will happen in your case.'

After they were dismissed, Precious approached Aunt Najiara, her father's youngest sister, the favourite and most liberal. 'What do you think they will ask me to do? Where should I go? I have no home of my own or outstanding dowry.' Precious asked.

'Your mother has missed you. Use this opportunity to spend time with her .I'll go with you when the elders summon you, so don't worry.'

Chapter 4: Confrontations
Coming to terms with the Past

'As for you Precious, you know the shame you brought to the family and your father's sadness and humiliation. You must come and meet with me and other clan elders to discuss what will happen in your case.'

Those words of Uncle Moses left Precious feeling vulnerable and anxious. Guilt weighed heavily on her with her father dying before she resolved the unforgiveness and cloud that overshadowed them. Once everyone had gone to bed Precious headed for her mother's bedroom with an urge to cuddle up to her like she used to do when she was young and scared. She loved to coil at the bottom of the bed like a ball. She gently knocked on the door a quiet voice said,

'Come in'

Kioni didn't know who was at the door that late; it was dark and lights already turned off; 'It's me mum; can I get into the bed? I can't seem to be able to go to sleep.'

'Of course *'Omukhana wo Mwami'* chief's daughter!' was accompanied by a sad smile.

'Do you remember when I was young I used to get into your bed in the morning and you would tell me to be silent until you finished praying because you had relatives around the world you wanted to pray for before you got out of bed in the morning. Now I am one of those relatives.'

They both giggled.

'I'd tuck myself at the bottom and keep silent until I heard you say 'Amen' then I would start asking questions.'

'Can I ask you some questions just l like I did as a child? Sometimes you got really annoyed with all my 'Why's' and 'What's'. If you don't like what I am going to ask you can shoo me away like you did then.'

'Mum, why did you and dad not share a room? Tell me about dad what sort of relationship did you two have?

'Your father was in his twenties and an orphan and I was only 15 when we married. At first we were friends. He knew I was young and playful and he allowed me to be myself and to grow into the marriage. I had to; I had no choice, I had to fall in love and as he was the adult I had to rely on him. Those days when you married you had no choice but to love the person so I did until he married the other women.

'When I gave birth to Blessing with the same reaction and response that I had for Mosi from the Chief, I told myself, "He is my husband and I still love him." He needed a son and blamed me for not giving him one. Mosi was often sick with malaria and watching her he feared that if even if he had a son, he could get sick and die and there would be instability.

'I understood but I cried myself to sleep when he told me that he is taking a second wife. I was raised by missionaries and believe strongly that man and woman should be one. He wasn't a Christian, he told me, so he could take more wives.

'As he grew in power because of his relationship with the British he repeated over and over the story of the white queen and talked fondly of this magical place where he watched her being crowned. I thought that if a woman can be head of the largest empire in world surely I can have ambitions for my daughters.

Once he married again our relationship changed. He told me he couldn't show his love to me openly because the other wives would be jealous and harm me and my children,'

'What do you mean, mum?'

'Do you understand witchcraft?'

'No not really; I don't believe in witchcraft. What harm could they have done?'

'Well I do and it could have meant you might have never finished school or they could have poisoned me. You are probably right but at the time it felt threatening. I was sad that I never gave him the first son he so needed and wanted; but I have no regrets because my daughters have made me proud.

'When I got pregnant with you the other two wives laughed saying that I was too old to carry a baby and when you were born, my darling, your father refused to name you because you were yet another girl.'

'Why did dad never show any affection towards us the girls or even you but treated the boys as if they were so special?'

'A lot of that is cultural – that's how the Tanga people treat the boys differently from girls. But your father cared and loved you all in private. He used to say "my poor daughters the world is big and wide and I worry when they marry they will suffer poor girls *'eshisira mbere'* "- the men might not treat them well.

'Why then did he expect me to marry someone I didn't really know or love? Why was he prepared to sell me?'

'My daughter that's tradition; his hands were tied. His anger was a mixture of shame and frustration that no one had told him the truth.

'Let me tell you something that has helped me to forgive him. When your father started ailing and became bedridden and on his death bed, he called me to the main house one early morning and asked everyone to leave us alone. He regretted that he had never apologised for the years he had been unkind to me and my children. That was the first time that I heard the word 'sorry' cross his lips'

'I'll never have that discussion with him now? It's too late. I know I got you into trouble and really hurt you and dad and put shame on the family but I had to do what was right for me at the time. I didn't want to be forced into a marriage like you or trapped in a loveless marriage. I am so sorry that you suffered so much because of me.'

Gentle tears started to flow down Precious's cheeks and Kioni took a handkerchief and wiped them away.

'I have forgiven you my daughter and understand why you did it. At the time I was beaten and sent home to my mother who had to suffer some ridicule and gossip. I felt sorry for you and bore it without complaint because I wanted what is best for you. I know you were always ambitious.'

'So what do I tell Uncle Moses and the elders tomorrow?'

'I taught you to be honest and true to yourself *Mwanawanje* my dear daughter. Answer truthfully what you are asked and avoid any confrontation or emotional tantrum, remember at the moment the timing is terrible everyone's emotionally on edge therefore more sensitive.'

"Yes mother."

'It is good to see you again after so long. I worried about you especially when there were big gaps between letters. I didn't know if you were alive or dead. The internet has been a blessing. I felt connected to you for the first time in years. You are looking happier. So what's your relationship with the white man? Are you sure he is just a friend as you say? You know you can tell me the truth; are you in love with him? I was watching you earlier and the way you were looking at him I know you well enough all I could see is love in your eyes. He actually has lovely legs.'

'Mum you can't say that; why have you been looking at his legs?

'Can't help it, can I when they are white and in a pair of shorts?

As they laughed together, Precious felt relaxed for the first time since she had come back home

'Let's try and sleep we have so much to do tomorrow and it won't be nice if people heard us giggling when we have a funeral. *'kata mumasika abaandu bachekhanga';* anyway even at funerals people are allowed to laugh;

The next morning Precious's half -sisters departed for their respective marital homes to perform the ritual as they have been instructed. The exceptions were Nechesa, who was here with her husband from Uganda Otieno, and Aluna, whose husband had died of AIDs three years earlier. Aluna had a good job in Nairobi and had chosen not to marry again.

Precious introduced Adrian to extended family members but not honestly. In Luhyia she said he was a journalist friend who would write about her father and about life in the village. Her cousin Paul's English was good and he volunteered to introduce Adrian to some elders, who he could interview on the past, present and future.

∞

Precious found a corner where she was able to access her emails without drawing attention to herself. She was surprised to see one from the Amahs.

'We want to ensure that Abeo's death will have a legacy and for it to be a reminder of the consequences of allowing the African and Afro Caribbean communities to be divided. We also want to remember the happy, smiling boy who was Abeo and his love of learning. Will you and Adrian help us please? We are in Ghana come to bury our son's ashes but will return to London in January. Can we meet then to get your opinion?'

Precious slept little that night too many thoughts spiralled in her head, Abeo's little body, his ashes and the gathering of the tribe in Tusanda, Kioni, Uncle Moses, Adrian, marriage … it was all too much

Chapter 5: Precious is summoned.
Educated women don't have dreadlocks

Summoned to appear under the big mango tree in the centre of the compound, Precious's embarrassment was undisguised. Every funeral goer was in the vicinity. Mourners were arriving all the time, wailing and bearing chickens. Precious guessed they would be surprised and curious to see her standing in the middle of a group of elders. Uncle Moses, of course, was centre stage.

Their eyes scanned Precious from head to toe. She guessed their thoughts from their expressions. 'Educated women don't have their hair in that style unless they are trying to make a statement.' Her dreadlocks were regarded as a sign of rebellion.

Precious was grateful that Aunt Najiara was by her side.

Uncle Moses banged his stick three times before beginning. 'Why does he do that?' thought Precious anxiously, but outwardly she tried to smile.

Moses greeted them in the traditional way and the elders answered in unison. Precious's palms started to sweat. Her feet felt numb, and she wanted the ground to swallow her up.

'We gather here under this mango tree in hard times and good times, but this is a difficult time. Everyone stand, and bang your sticks to the ground three times in honour of our beloved chief, my brother.'

When the noise died down, Moses looked with distain at Precious.

'You will remember Precious Lutta, Kioni's daughter.'

The elders mumbled under their breath. 'You all remember the circumstances in which she left Tusanda. I am pleased she has sufficient dignity to attend her father's funeral, but I have called her to this meeting to seek your advice and wisdom.

No girl before her has fled and refused a marriage arranged by the elders, bringing shame to our family. More pressing is the matter of the family of Omollo whom she refused to marry. How do we deal with the issue? They will attend the funeral and if they know she is still not married they have the right to claim her.'

Aunt Najiara stood up and greeted them. Slowly and respectfully, she said,

'It is your duty to protect our chief's daughter. She's in mourning. It would not be right to accept any gifts from Omollo's family during this time. And it would be inappropriate for them to raise the matter.'

The elders muttered between themselves looking none too pleased. They decided that the matter could be postponed on those grounds to be discussed after the funeral. Precious was dismissed.

Precious glanced gratefully in the direction of her aunt but it didn't stop her feeling like an outcast. If the worst came to the worst after the funeral she could leave – she could run away. But run where? There were so many problems waiting for her in London but for the moment she could forget them.

Osundwa

Adrian and Precious were sitting outside when a smart 4X4 pulled up and out stepped a distinguished looking man in his fifties. Mama Murono ran as fast as her weight allowed her and hugged her son.

'Who's that?' asked Adrian.

'It must be the new chief. Osundwa went to study law at Chicago. He returned once when I was at boarding school and again with his wife in 2004 but then I was in Uganda. He met his wife in America, but she's from Ghana. He has a fine career as a professor. Will he want to succeed my father and be chief?'

That evening, Adrian and Precious sat under a tree in quiet companionship. They didn't feel like talking. After years living in a city, they tried to listen to the sounds of nature rather than the human voice. It slowed down the rhythms of the body and relaxed them both.

Their silence was broken when Osundwa came over to them and held out his hand.

'You must be Precious, and this is…?' His tone was friendly and his handshake firm. He smiled at Precious and waited to be introduced to Adrian

'Adrian Harris. I'm a journalist from London. You must be the new chief?

'Well, therein lies a problem.'

He turned to Precious, 'I heard from my mother about your ordeal yesterday. You have my sympathy. How do you think they'll take it when I tell them I don't want to be their chief?

Precious raised her already arched eyebrows even higher.

'What a break with tradition that will be! Does that mean Samuel will succeed our father?

'I'd better go and talk to Moses. I could consider taking on the role in four or five years' time when our children are at university. Then I'll be able to take a sabbatical. But even then I wouldn't want to spend all my time here. My home is in Illinois. At least part of me is always there.'

The next morning the village was abuzz with rumour. In a break with tradition the new chief would not be crowned after the funeral. Uncle Moses was to be regent until Osundwa was ready to take over.

Osundwa came to Precious to give her the news.

'Moses likes the idea of being regent and has agreed with me that they will forgive and forget the past. There'll be no more interrogations and reprimands. You are free to mourn father like the rest of us.'

Precious sighed with relief and thought that America had changed her half- brother for the better.

The Day of the Funeral

Adrian woke to a commotion and the sound of wailing. He looked out to see a procession of men accompanied by bulls and women carrying bags of maize. Everyone wore black. Precious had warned him and he had brought suitable clothes. He dressed quickly and dashed outside to join the procession.

They were shown where to sit and told who would address the mourners. Adrian was sent to join the men.

As Kioni was the first wife, she was the first to speak. Despite all her suffering, her speech was emotional and moving. The same could not be said of what came next. Speech after speech followed and Precious sighed.

'Speeches go on for so long,' she whispered to Nechesa who was sat next to her. She was unsettled by her inability to concentrate. Despite trying hard to focus her thoughts back into her tribal culture, her attention kept slipping and after a while she stopped listening. In the void, her mind travelled from London to Tusanda to Uganda and back to the day of the dowry. She shivered with a horrible feeling that her father had not forgiven her. Through the heat haze, Nechesa noticed her tremble.

There was a loud screech of brakes as a white four-wheel-drive vehicle entered the compound right in front of the seated crowd. A man in sharp tailored black clothes and dark glasses jumped out and scanned the crowd before opening the passenger door. Bright shiny shoes appeared and everyone fell silent, uncertain who this important guest could be. As he turned towards them, their faces contorted with expressions of disgust.

'Who is that?' Precious asked Nechesa.

'He's the MP. How disrespectful of him to drive right in front of us and not park his car in the designated area. How can he afford a Mercedes and surround himself with all those bodyguards when his people are so poor? I hope they'll stand up to him and deny him a slot to speak—crashing in as if he's more important than our father.'

After a long sermon by the Bishop, the local MP was invited to say something.

'While you are all gathered together, I wanted to tell you my plans for this community.' He talked about building a road, a bridge and new classrooms. Precious waited for him to pay tribute to her father and express his condolences to his family, but nothing came.

After a few heart-rending songs from the choir and performances by the traditional dancers, the crowd followed the coffin to the graveside. They processed in order of birth: the wives at the front, followed by the children from oldest to youngest walking in pairs. Four seats were provided for all the wives to sit down while the final reading and burial service was carried out.

'Dust to dust, ashes to ashes…' intoned the bishop. Kioni started sobbing. Precious had never seen her cry before. Adrian had been allowed to take photographs of the choir and dancers and speeches but now he put his camera down.

That evening, sitting in the courtyard, he showed some to Precious.

'You're good, you know—a good photographer, I mean.'

Adrian looked pleased.

Nechesa's husband Otieno came over to take a look. The two men liked each other immediately. Otieno took Adrian by the arm and they walked together to where the men were gathering.

'I find this patriarchy as hard to take as you do,' he said.

'Precious tried to warn me that rural Kenya is conservative, but I hadn't a clear idea of what that meant. I'm still confused. I know how traumatic it was for her leaving Kenya and running away from an arranged marriage. But I assume your marriage was arranged, and you and Nechesa seem to have a modern relationship. How is that? Sorry' he added, 'I'm being a nosey journalist.'

'Officially our marriage was arranged but in reality, it wasn't.'

'Now you're confusing me even more!'

'Let me explain. Nechesa and I met at Makarere University in Uganda. I didn't want a traditional marriage. Nechesa is my equal. We had good conversations, often challenging ones. At first, they upset me, but when we were apart, I missed them, and I missed her! As you say, this is a conservative society, but we worked out a way. I persuaded my parents to come with me to Tusanda to see the chief and officially ask for her hand. Chief Kidake liked the idea that I had graduated; he held a degree from Makarere in high esteem. My parents went 'through the motions', which I believe is the correct phrase. They negotiated with him and the elders. You could say that we conned them into thinking it was a traditional arranged marriage, even if it was a bit unusual as it hadn't involved a wanjira.' He smiled at Adrian's blank expression. 'A wanjira is a go-between, someone to negotiate between the two families. That was how I married the girl I loved. I feel lucky.'

Adrian pressed him further, 'Even though you had the traditional ceremony at least Nechesa wasn't sold off to the highest bidder?'

'But my family still had to pay a dowry.' Otieno replied. Adrian looked aghast. 'I agree, it's ridiculous, but I had to do it to make her parents happy. When our daughters get married, we won't make their husband pay a dowry. Hopefully in the next couple of generations, the practice will disappear.'

Adrian looked on thoughtfully. The idea of having to buy Precious, even to make her extended family happy, appalled him. But he understood why Otieno and Nechesa had gone through with it. He hoped Otieno was right and the practice would die out with the older generation.

While Adrian chatted to Otieno, Precious found a quiet corner where she could check her emails. There was a friendly message from Katie. She hesitated for a moment before opening one from Inspector Ball. For him to email her – it was not good news.

'There has been another incident. The location was the bus stop on Victoria Road near the Methodist Church. This time the unlucky target didn't get away and is in St Thomas's hospital. He's lucky that the knife missed an artery. The CCTV footage is unclear but the gang look to be wearing bandanas of the type Nelson wears. There is not sufficient evidence to charge him and the victim is afraid and doesn't want to testify. The importance of you as a witness to Abeo's murder and the incident in Notting Hill can't be over stated. We are working hard to build a case. When you get back from Kenya, come and see me.

Aluna interrupted her.

'Sister, why so glum?' She beckoned to Nechesa to join them and then

whispered, 'Tonight the men will perform some rituals they like to keep secret. Let's have some fun. Let's hide and watch.'

Precious welcomed the distraction and the women sneaked through the compound. A blaze of flames penetrated the darkness. A group of elders, all men, were gathered by the grave. Uncle Moses slaughtered a rooster and put it on the fire to roast. Aluna and Precious watched as they chanted. From a distance the words sounded like whispers. Precious asked Nechesa.

'Why a rooster?'

'Superstitious people believe that if a rooster stands on one leg in the homestead it is inviting death on the head of the home. People who are afraid kill the rooster and eat it as a preventative measure.'

Nechesa started to recall other superstitious customs with mock seriousness.

'Do you remember the cooking stones in the kitchen? One represents
your father, one your mother and one the children. Father's stone will have to be removed as it could lead to a curse and even death. There's even a ritual called 'sexual cleansing' before starting a sex life again after the death of a husband or wife.'

'I haven't heard of that one. What's that about?' asked Precious.

'The widow is required to travel to a faraway place and find a male stranger who will make love to her without revealing to the man that she is a widow.'

'What if someone finds them?' asked Precious.

'The woman only has to accept foreplay with her new lover.'

'What happens when it comes to intercourse?' asked Precious.

'Perhaps she'll scream saying something has bitten her or that somebody is coming and they will both run away,' suggested Aluna who then asked,

'What if they are in a lodge? What happens then?'

Nechesa giggled and said, 'I haven't worked that one out. Maybe that's why Uncle Moses is so opposed to staying in a hotel. Do you think he believes that sexual cleansing has taken place in the rooms.'

'Why is it only women who have to sexually cleanse?' asked Precious.

'Oh no, it's both genders. It symbolically frees the woman from being a wife and the man from being a husband. There are stories that put the fear of God into women though. The gossip is that if she doesn't go through with the ritual, any children from a future relationship will be strange creatures. Have you seen any of those strange creatures?'

Precious giggled. 'Maybe the man my father wanted me to marry was one of them?' They burst into laughter.

'Stop that noise!' shouted Aunt Nanjira who came out of her house and saw them. Aluna put a finger to her lips but she grinned and carried on whispering.

'Just to warn you, bereaved family members must be shaved on the third day after burial to rid themselves of 'breath of death' caused by their association with the deceased.'

'No way am I getting my head shaved. Do you know how long it's taken me to grow it this long, not to mention the hours I've spent braiding it?

'So what are you going to tell Uncle Moses?'

Precious raised her eyebrows and shrugged her shoulders.

'Do you know why there are so many children in the village who are named after grandfather's cousin?' Nechesa said into the silence.

'No, why is that?' Precious asked.

'After the burial, the clan members are urged to strive to give birth and name their children after the deceased. I bet there'll be lots of children named after our father.'

Nechesa nudged Precious. 'You and Adrian need to think about that too.'

∞

The next day Nechesa and Precious headed down to the river together. Precious was unusually quiet and Nechesa waited until she was sure that the two of them were out of earshot before she spoke more freely.

'I didn't mean to embarrass you last night, Precious. I'm sorry if what I said offended you.'

'No, don't apologise! It's my fault. You're right about how I feel about Adrian, but I find being home so stressful that I can't deal with introducing him as my future husband along with everything else that's going on.'

'Future husband?' Nechesa stopped in her tracks and pulled Precious around to face her, kicking up dust from the force of her actions.

'He asked me to marry him on the way here,' Precious said quietly.

'But this is great news!' Nechesa was exuberant. We have to tell Mama, she'll be so happy. I'm sure she'll love Adrian once she gets to know him. He's such a kind and thoughtful man.'

Precious didn't say anything but looked down at her feet and twisted her toes into the dry mud.

'What's wrong,' said Nechesa, exasperated. 'You've just told me you're engaged to this amazing man who's flown halfway around the world to meet your family, and you look miserable.'

'People will think I'm a prostitute.' Precious said even more quietly than before.

Nechesa laughed. She knew it was unkind, but Precious was never normally so glum and insecure, and what she'd said was so completely ridiculous.

'Let me tell you a story that Otieno told me,' said Nechesa grabbing Precious's hand and pulling her along the path again. 'It's a true story about the first recorded legal marriage between a Kenyan man and a white woman. It was 1955, colonial times...' Nechesa adopted a grandiose tone in her 'Queen's English', as if she was beginning an epic tale. Precious couldn't help but give a small smile. It reminded

111

her of when they were children and Nechesa and she had whispered stories to each other to help them fall asleep in the cramped bed.

'Their names were John Kimuyu and Ruth Holloway. She was a white missionary and he was not just black but also blind. Racism was vicious. The independence movement was in its brutal seventh year and the British colonialists declared an emergency to crush the Mau Mau.'

'I didn't know about them' said Precious 'but I watched the film *A United Kingdom*. That was about the Chief of Botswana. The British exiled Seretse Khama for marrying Ruth Williams, a white woman, and she was not welcome in Africa. But they were brave. They had a good marriage and the people came to love her.' Nechesa nudged Precious gently.

'It doesn't matter if some people here don't like it. All that matters is that you love each other.'

Precious didn't say anything but after a while she glanced up from her feet and held her head high in the manner of Kioni.

'Thank you, Nechesa,' Precious said finally, 'I'm sorry I've not been myself. Being with you—being here—has brought back uncomfortable feelings including an urge to run away. I thought I'd overcome it and that I knew what I wanted, but all this talk of children is unsettling me. Do you remember when I fled to Uganda?'

'What a silly question! How could I forget? It took father a long time to forgive me for helping you.'

'I don't think I ever thanked you properly either,' whispered Precious.

'No you didn't and I don't think you thanked Jairus either. You do remember Jairus who organised your escape?

'He left soon after you. His friend Mohammed came for the funeral. He's heard from him. Jairus is living in the States.'

'Could you get his email address for me? I need to thank him. Jairus had a vehicle waiting at the bottom of the farm hoping no one would find out and stymie the whole plan. I'm glad he wasn't caught, but I feel guilty for not asking about what happened to him or thanking him properly.'

'You had other things on your mind, Precious. '

'But it's bad. I shouldn't be so forgetful. I didn't forget but got caught up in my struggle for survival. It's selfish I know, but my urge for autonomy didn't allow much time for niceties.'

'I'm sure he doesn't blame you.'

'He gave me such good advice. He told me to travel light, but said I could pass a small bag of clothes to his sister cousin. I put the bag in a bucket, and pretended I was going to feed the chickens and took it to her.

'Early the next morning, before mum woke up, I pretended I was going to the toilet at the bottom of the compound near the gate.'

'But you did have some money with you, didn't you?' said Nechesa.

'Yeah, but my savings weren't enough to pay for the journey all the way to Jinja. Jairus didn't charge me for taking me to the Ugandan border. He reminded me to take my ID because I couldn't cross the border without it. Remind me of how you knew I was coming? It would be so easy now—we could just use mobile phones.'

'A shop keeper called Baraza bought his supplies in Kenya every week and was happy to do our personal errands like delivering and collecting letters and small parcels. That's why we all called him 'the post man'. He delivered Jairus's letter explaining what was happening and when I should expect you. I was so worried and afraid of what would happen if you were stopped at the border or caught.'

'You know that the journey to the border takes only an

hour. But that day, it felt like forever. I was worried that I was being followed. My anxiety led to a kind of panic attack. It felt as if I couldn't breathe, but Jairus had thought of everything. He told the driver to carry other passengers on the way so that it looked like a normal journey, so we picked up a few people going to the markets. Some had chickens, some vegetables and most couldn't stop talking which was a great distraction. One of the ladies said she was a fish trader who got her supplies from Uganda.

'I knew that she could help me cross the border, so I started to talk to her. She was so kind. I still remember her name, Auma. She showed me exactly what to do and invited me to follow her, which I did. She greeted a few officials at customs. They seemed to know her well and before long we were through! Even inside Uganda, I was still nervous. I resisted the urge to run but with every step I expected that someone would call me back. Auma walked with me to a rowdy bus stop and showed me which matatu would take me to Kampala. Once I jumped into the matatu, I was so relieved. I could breathe. I finally felt safe. But thoughts of mum and how she would feel when they couldn't find me cut my mind. I guessed that she'd be blamed. I was worried Uncle Moses wouldn't be kind to her. Do you know if dad defended her or accused of being a bad woman?'

'You know the answer to that. But she has forgiven you. I'm not sure that I have,' said Nechesa looking stern.

'I am so sorry. Really I am,' said Precious.

Nechesa's face creased with laughter lines.

'Well you fell for that one and it was half true so now I can forgive you.'

Nechesa didn't mention the letter she had received from her father.

Nechesa ,

I was asked to go to Sumo to mediate a land dispute that's been causing fights for years. The detail is tedious and sometimes it's one word against another as old colonial records, the only reliable source of information, offer proof of only a few claims. Sometimes people go to the lengths of paying bribes to falsify the evidence. In this case the two parties finally came to a compromise and I was at last able to return home.

The sight of the old mango tree put me in a good mood. I was welcomed by my wives and settled contentedly in my chair while they went in to prepare my lunch. While I waited, I sent for Precious thinking that it is good having an educated daughter who follows current affairs. Your uncle Moses doesn't understand why I discuss these matters with a woman—and a young one at that—but she has good sense and pragmatism. I even thought that she could make a good chief if she were not a woman.

Peter came to greet me. When I asked where Precious was, he told me she'd left home a week ago. When Kioni brought my lunch, I demanded to know where she'd gone. She hadn't asked my permission to leave. Kioni didn't reply. I felt so angry that I threw down the calabash and it smashed on the ground, lumps of brown porridge flying in every direction soiling my robes. Kioni bent down to pick up the pieces but said nothing.

I shouted at her and told her how humiliating Precious's disappearance would be when the Omollo family arrive next week, hoping to meet the future bride. She didn't utter a word. That must mean she knows all too well but is not prepared to tell me. I can't bear to see her face. I can't trust myself. I can't be sure what I will do. I believe Precious is with you. Send her back now

115

and I will not blame you or your mother.'

'Ade, I don't know what to do. Uncle Moses is a stickler for following tradition. Like a Sadducee in the Bible, he sees it as his duty to enforce the rituals down to the last detail. Normally after a chief's death all married daughters must return to their marital homes, but unmarried family like me and close friends are expected to stay in the compound for seven days without leaving. If you stay here with me, you'll be bored out of your mind, but if I leave before the seven days are up, I'll be persona non grata all over again.'

'You must stay and stop worrying. I'll find ways of occupying myself.'

'You don't get many holidays, Adrian. Aluna has a friend who takes people on safari in the Masai Mara. It's not that far. With that camera of yours, you'll love it. Go off for five days and enjoy yourself. When you return, we'll spend a day here and you can get to know my mother. For the next few days she won't be in the right mood. Then we'll have to leave.'

Precious could see that Adrian liked the idea but was reluctant to admit it, so she went ahead and organised it. At noon the next day, Aluna's friend arrived with a Nissan 4x4.

'Off you go now. You'll never forget it. You can't come to Kenya without at least a small safari.'

Adrian didn't protest too much. Precious waved goodbye from the doorway.

'How lucky Samuel came home for the funeral,' she thought. 'He's an experienced safari guide and speaks French as well as English. He's a great animal photographer, perfect company for Adrian.'

After he left Precious visited the grave. She found herself talking to her father. 'I did love you, Dad. You had so many problems to deal with. I'm sorry you looked on me as just another one.'

There was so much she left unsaid, but after the emotional draining week she didn't have the strength to go on. She threw a handful of flowers on to the grave and as if in response a leaf fluttered down from the overhanging tree. She'd appeased her dad's spirit. Peace came over her as wingbeats from the waxbill which had disturbed the branch calmed the noise in her head. This was gentle – not the flight in panic which had informed her life so far. This simple ritual closed a chapter in her life.

Chapter 6: News from England
Sisters on a narrow bridge

Wifi connection was erratic but until now it had felt good to be cut off from screens. Precious kept checking her phone. Adrian had promised he would text if he could. She was surprised to see a message not from him but from Darrel.

'Sorry to be the bearer of bad news. Inspector Ball asked me to let you know. They've found CCTV footage that puts Nelson and Jacob in the area of Abeo's murder and have charged them. It's good that you're in Kenya.'

She had been able to put the threats behind her, separated as she was by thousands of miles of land and sea, and moving in with Adrian and the funeral had occupied her mind. She'd tried so hard not to let the attack change her behaviour, but remembering it now she couldn't help herself. Her hand trembled as she stared at the message. She tried to console herself with, 'Nelson and Jacob are teenage tearaways who didn't mean to kill Abeo.'

Her rational self knew she was being deliberately naive. The garden had denied the Wolf Crew a prime location for their dealing. The gang leaders, two hardened and ruthless guys in their mid-twenties, must have felt that their territory was under threat.

'Had they ordered Nelson and Jacob to wound Abeo as a punishment, or had they intended his execution?'

Unbeknown to Precious, Nechesa had been watching and saw her agitation.

She came over and put an arm around her. 'Let's sit on the rocks by the river like we used to as children.'

'Has this river shrunk?' Nechesa asked, as they arrived at the bank. 'Or am I just older and have seen bigger rivers? When we were children this river seemed so fast and deep.'

'Maybe you're right, but there's been little rain so perhaps it could just be a bit shallow from the dry season,' Precious replied.

They crossed the narrow, unstable wooden bridge.

'Gosh you need good balance and yet women cross this fragile wooden bridge with baskets balanced on their heads from the market. Why is it nearly always the women who do the heavy lifting?' Then, embarrassed, she added, 'Ignore me Nechesa.'

'There's our favourite rock. It hasn't changed at all.' said Nechesa. 'How beautiful to be here after all these years. Can you hear the frogs and the crickets? Look at that dragonfly! It's iridescent in the sun. I adore its kingfisher blue colours. Talking of kingfishers, look over there!'

Precious grinned. Nechesa had succeeded in lightening her mood.

'I wish I'd thanked you at the time for hosting me when I needed to run away.'

'It wasn't for long. Once you got that scholarship you didn't hang around.'

'But it was you who boosted my confidence and encouraged me to start looking at scholarship opportunities in the US. I wanted better opportunities, but I was scared Father would send men after me if I stayed with you in Uganda. I managed to make contact with people I knew at a university in London.'

'Why did you want to go to London and not the States? I've forgotten the reason.'

'Odd, isn't it? It was Father's decision to marry me off to the highest bidder that made me flee Tusanda, and it was Father's description of England that made me want to move there. Do you remember how he painted this amazing picture of London? When I was offered the scholarship to do a Masters at Westminster University, it was like heading for the moon.

'Oginga Odinga, who went to study in London, agreed to invite me as his guest and sponsor me so long as I could cover my air ticket. He accommodated me for a few weeks until I could find work and a place of my own. He put a lot of emphasis on "few"'. She chuckled quietly.

'Good Lord, it's all coming back to me now! But we still had a problem, do you remember? You hadn't earned enough in three months to cover the cost of your flight,' said Nechesa.

'Yes, and you and Otieno covered all my living costs and took a loan to help me cover the balance. I owe you a lot, my dear sister. You've been my rock. I can't even believe you're here with me now. I'm going through a tough experience in London.'

'It's a long time since we had a heart-to-heart chat. We haven't talked like this since I waved goodbye to my little sister at the airport eight years ago. But I still know when things are not right. Are you going to tell me what's wrong?'

It felt a huge relief talking about it. At some points in the story Nechesa looked confused.

'Father taught us to think of London like some well-governed Utopia but what you're telling me makes me appreciate what we have—children who respect their elders,' said Nechesa.

'Boys like Nelson often don't know their fathers. They abandoned them at birth or, at best, call in from time to time. Boys like Nelson often have siblings fathered by other men who treat the mother the same. They don't have loving men in their lives. They look up to the guys who have money, handsome clothes, smart cars and respect. They are groomed and flattered by the apparent friendship of these older men—that's why they join gangs. Then it becomes their identity. If they want out, they are scared for their lives,' said Precious.

'Do you think that if they had a strong male role model

who insisted on acting for the good of the group then they wouldn't go over to the dark side?' asked Nechesa, who'd watched Star Wars on a DVD.

'What do you mean? They need an Uncle Moses to keep them in line?' asked Precious, and for the first time in days a proper smile crossed her face.

They returned to the house arm-in-arm only to see Samuel and Adrian arriving at the compound.

'Why are you back so early? I wasn't expecting you until Wednesday night,' said a surprised Precious.

'We stopped at an internet café yesterday. There was an email from Delroy. George—Dad—they admitted him to St Thomas' three days ago. Delroy thinks I should hurry home. It's lung cancer. I'm so sorry Precious—I have to go. Under the circumstances, they've brought my flight forward with only a small penalty. I hope you don't mind?' Adrian looked worried as he spoke.

'Of course I don't mind. Oh Ade, I hope Delroy is wrong. Perhaps they have caught it in time? But you must be with him. He'll be afraid.'

Adrian gave Precious a big hug, oblivious to the onlookers. Precious felt eyes on her. Her secret was out. Uncle Moses had been watching.

As they broke apart Uncle Moses continued to glare at them. Precious caught his eye and he spat on the ground, muttering just loudly enough for her to hear.

'How can you prostitute yourself in front of family? Have you no shame?'

Unaware, Adrian smiled as he shook hands and said his goodbyes. He and Samuel got back in the Nissan and headed off in the direction of Kisumu for the next flight to Nairobi. She watched as the car disappeared, enveloped in a cloud of dust. Precious felt bereft and knew that she wanted and needed Adrian in her life. But anxiety overwhelmed her.

Chapter 7: Going Through Kidake's papers
Understanding the past: Worried about the future

On the seventh day, Precious was woken by a piercing wail. She put on her black mourning dress, covered her head with a headscarf and hurried out, wondering what could have happened to be confronted with the sight of her father's worldly possessions placed on his grave.

She sighed as she remembered that tradition demanded that her father's siblings, cousins and other close relatives took everything he owned—his clothes, walking stick, three-legged stool, fly whisk, chief's uniforms, three gold bracelets and round colonial hat. All that was left on the grave were his textbooks and notebooks

Precious observed the hierarchy as his things were allocated. Uncle Moses had priority. He picked the three-legged stool and the three gold bracelets.

The rest of her father's brothers and their cousins picked all the nice things, leaving only what they felt was of no value.

'How unfair. What about us?' Precious whispered to her mother. 'His children and wives. Have we no entitlement to his belongings?'

Kioni said simply, 'We come into this world with nothing and leave the earth with nothing.'

Kioni and the other wives were each given a rooster, a big cooking pot, a calabash and a rope from the family bulls and told their responsibility now was to look after the rest of the family. The gifts symbolised the women's duty to make sure that all the guests to the chief's home were fed and protected.

Later, Kioni explained to Precious that the things handed down from her grandfather were not to be touched by women and a woman was not allowed to sit on the three-legged stool.

'It is rumoured that the three gold bracelets were brought from Egypt by our ancestors. Egypt is thought to be our family's place of origin,' said Kioni.

Aluna looked angry. Precious glanced towards her enquiringly and Aluna whispered, 'This is the seventh day and one of our uncles will inherit Kioni and Murono.'

'No! Surely not in the twenty-first century?' said Precious. 'Treated like father's clothes, jewellery and stool, like just another piece of property?'

'Our mother is made of strong stuff. Kioni will refuse to be inherited.'

As the women left the graveside, Precious's cousin told them the story of a neighbour who had refused to be inherited by her brother-in-law. She knew that his wife had died of AIDS. She was chased away from the village and now lived in the slums of Ekero.

Precious needed to be with her mother. When she arrived back at the house, it was still full of mourners. It was not until everyone else had gone to bed that Precious could share her fears with her mother.

Kioni hugged her daughter. 'Have no fear, Precious Lutta. Times are changing even here. I won't be "inherited". Older women like me are not expected to practise such traditions not any more.'

Precious looked relieved but forged on.

'I need to talk to you about Adrian.'

Kioni smiled at her daughter. That smile told Precious that her mother had already guessed the truth.

'I want you to be happy. I am sorry I had so little time with him but I heard from others how respectful he is.'

∞

Osundwu sent for Precious and Nechesa. He was in their father's office surrounded by boxes of files. He indicated the mountain of scrapbooks, old newspapers, legal documents and correspondence and then put his head in his hands.

'I have to leave not long after you two, and I have no idea what to do with all this.'

Precious and Nechesa had not been in their father's private sanctum before and were surprised by just how many files there were.

'Let's send for a drink and discuss what to do and then the three of us can set about sorting them out,' suggested Nechesa.

While they sipped their beer, Nechesa picked up a scrapbook lying on the floor and couldn't believe what she was seeing. Here was an account of her father's coronation followed by pictures of him at the Coronation of Queen Elizabeth II. In that picture he was wearing a well-tailored three-piece suit but draped over it was a leopard skin. He looked impressive in his chief's hat.

She handed around his description of his own coronation. After reading it they were all silent for a while. They had never thought of their father, Kidake, as an individual. To them he had always been the chief defined by his role.

The blood of the bulls soaked the ground. Those red drops sting like tears for my father. I am not ready. I thought he would live to be an old man not leave his son so soon before he could pass on his wisdom to me. I am not prepared for the responsibility of becoming chief. The timing feels ominous like those Greek myths I was taught at the missionary school. Given that I have no love for the people who claim to rule over us and have the power to enslave us, why do I feel akin to this young Queen? The day her father died she was pronounced Queen. Does anyone understand what that means better than I who am sharing that experience? She at least can dry her tears before going through the rituals.

I must have a wife. Elizabeth II has a consort whom she can lean on. The fifteen year old girl, this daughter of a pastor, they have chosen for me –how can she help me?

I must swear allegiance to my tribe –the Tanga people whose origins are in this land that straddles what is now called Kenya and Uganda. Our British rulers ignore this. They have divided us and separated us from our land – that land that gave us life. At twenty two years of age how will I negotiate this treacherous river?

This morning instead of heading for the USA to study, I sat upon the stool of power and was dressed in the leopard skin robes of a chief. On my head they placed the headgear which will mark me out as I travel. It is made from the fur of a Colobus monkey. In turn the elders placed in my hand the symbols of authority, the fly whisk, the walking stick, and the gold bracelet to be worn on my right arm. What the people will remember is the feast and the music and dancing and celebration of my late father and of me his son, Chief Kidake of the Tanga people.

Between them they spent the next two days sorting out the mess. Nechesa said, 'I'm curious about these letters and old newspapers. We mustn't throw them away. They are our history and I can't believe that I'm so ignorant of it. This correspondence – you do realise who it's between – President Barack Obama's father and our father! If you think about it, it's not so surprising. They went to the same school and like him our father was planning to go to the USA on Tom Mboya's scholarship. Then Grandfather died and he had his youth taken away from him.'

She pointed to the London Coronation photographs and said, 'rather like Queen Elizabeth.'

Osundwa nodded his agreement.

'Obama's father came back to Kenya in 1964. He became a

senior economist in the Kenyan Ministry of Finance. But he had qualifications from Harvard and our father lost out on his opportunity to do a PhD. That must have grated.'

'Father thought these letters were significant at the time or he wouldn't have kept copies of his own letters as well as Obama Sn's replies,' said Nechesa.

Osundwa was gazing intently at an official looking document.

'What's that about?' asked Precious.

'It's a notification of the funeral of his friend.'

'Of course Father would have gone to the funeral. Nyang'oma Kogelo, where Obama is buried is not far from Kisumu and the rituals would have been similar to what we've just experienced,' said Precious.

Osundwa nodded and continued,

'Obama Sn's prospects ended when Tom Mboya was assassinated. Mboya was a patron to our father too. Could Mboya's murder have cast a cloud over him? His friend turned to drink and was involved in two car crashes. Some even hint that the1982 crash which killed Obama was no accident.'

'Why didn't Father talk to us about this?' asked Nechesa.

'Perhaps he was protecting us? That could be the reason why he didn't get involved in national politics and was always lecturing us about doing our duty to our own people?' suggested Precious. She put out her hand to touch Usundwa who was holding a letter that had brought tears to his eyes.

'I had forgotten about this trip to Tanzania. Why? How could I have forgotten?' He handed the letter to Precious. It was dated 1969. She read it out loud.

"The news of Tom Mboya's murder sent me into a spiral of despair, and I didn't want the family or the tribe to see it. What happened to the hope we had at that party in his home in

126

1962? Tom helped my friend Barack Hussein Obama to get an education in the USA. That was what he hoped for me, but my father died before I could take advantage of the opportunity. Obama will need to keep his opinions to himself if he wants to survive but at least we have ways of sharing correspondence securely where we can be honest. I needed to get away so I accepted Mary and Louis Leakey's invitation to visit their excavations in Olduvai Gorge. I took my son Osundwa with me. I want him to be inspired. I picked up a handful of soil and let it fall through my fingers. I encouraged him to take home a fossil and said to him: 'All human life began in our homeland and spread across the earth. I want you to see the world that emigration has created and learn from it. Then you can return home and dig deep roots."

'I still have that fossil but from now on it will have pride of place on my desk', said Usundwa.

'It'll take a while to read all these,' said Nechesa pointing to the piles of correspondence. That evening she took one letter to Kioni. Her mother could speak enough English to be understood but because her education had been cut short, she could not read it. Nechesa felt she should share her father's letter to Barack Hussein Obama written in 1959.

"I brought Peter home. Kioni is overwhelmed to see her brother again, but the man who returns is not the same man who left. He is broken physically and mentally. He walks with a limp and his spirit is unrecognisable.

My decision to support the British means we have been spared the land confiscations that the Kikuyu people have suffered. Rumours circulated about the camps and the brutal conditions, about the barbed wire encircling villages where women were forced to work for white people. Kioni's family had believed that as Peter had fought for the British in the World War he would have been spared. Kioni is shell-shocked, she had no idea that he was in one of those camps.

Over the next few days he told me of his ordeal, the executions he witnessed and the torture inflicted on him. He spared me the details, but the effects were etched on his face and his skeletal body. Sometimes in the night I could hear his screaming across the compound. When I asked him how it happened, he told me the story of his imprisonment.

'I was visiting an old comrade from the war in Burma. He is Kikuyi and lived in the village Mathare, near Nairobi. It was the 24th April 1954, the day they launched Anvil.'

I nodded, I'd already heard from others about the British's violent suppression and incarceration of supporters of the Mau Mau uprising.

"Military vehicles with loudspeakers drove through the village. Everyone was confused and afraid; nobody knew what was going on. Those who moved slowly or too quickly were beaten with clubs. Anyone who protested at the rough handling was put in special vehicles and taken away. They handcuffed me and threw me in a lorry with fifty others. One man was suffocated on the journey to Langata camp.

"At the camp we were put in a line and made to walk past a person with a sack over his head with holes cut for eyes. As we walked past the person inside looked at each of us and if he nodded his head, he recognised you as Mau Mau, but if he shook it you were released. When they realised I was not Kikuyu, they said I would be released, but I complained about the treatment of my comrades from the war so they sent me to Hola Camp. I was accused of being a supporter of Mau Mau, and they tortured me to try and make me confess."

My heart knotted in sorrow when Peter told me he is one of the lucky ones. He has survived to tell the tale. I feel such a confusing mixture of emotions, mainly fury at the British. In my heart I feel they must leave Kenya. This is our land and they have no right to rule over us. I cannot believe that the young Queen I met only five years ago has allowed her people to treat us with such cruelty and disdain. My collaboration with them fills me with guilt. I'm doing what I can to protect my village and my family but how can I justify this when my inaction leads to the death and torture of so many others?"

'Mama, why didn't I know about this? Why was nothing said at his funeral? Only that he had fought for the British in Burma?' asked Nechesa.

Kioni shook her head.

'I'm sorry I don't know the answer to that. I didn't tell you because I thought we were heading for better times. Was I wrong thinking we should look onwards and upwards as if climbing to the summit of Kilimanjaro and not back to those dark and painful times?'

Kioni drew Nechesa to her in a warm maternal embrace.

'Thank you for reading that to me. It reminded me of the times your father thought of me with kind thoughts. I have tried to be strong for my daughters.'

In the morning she told Precious and Osundwa.

'Don't you think we need to talk about these things? Can we really know who we are without knowing about our family's past? It's so entwined with Kenya's history that surely it is important that we share it? I'd like to take the letters home with me and sort them out according to who was the recipient. Do you think Moses will let me?'

'I'll recommend it. It could be that the Presidential archive in the USA will be interested in this correspondence. When you are back in Jinja can you scan the most interesting ones and email them to me,' replied Osundwa.

'They'll interest Adrian. Don't forget he's a journalist. Can you copy him in to the emails please?' added Precious.

Chapter 8: Kioni finds a baby
A son at last

On her last night in Tusanda Precious found it hard to sleep. She had heard a whispered rumour about an abandoned three-month-old baby, but she doubted whether it was true. The thought of the tiny, lonely infant kept her awake until the early hours. The next morning, she confronted her mother. Kioni grinned.

'It's true. I found Joseph abandoned on my farm. He was probably only a couple of months old.'

'Another person who won't know when they're born,' Precious half joked.

A hint of sadness flickered across her face and Precious regretted her words.

'Tell me about him, Mum.'

'I can't wait to finish this funeral and pick him up from my sister's house. This is the best thing that has happened to me in a long time, finding that baby. I assumed it was my neighbour's child crying; she takes her daughter with her when she works in the fields. But when I heard the whimper coming from the same direction on the third day, I walked through the crops and found him. How had he survived? The skin on his back was raw and was being eaten by ants. He is my miracle—the son I never had. I have a sense of purpose again, Precious.'

'It reminds me of when I had Mosi,' Kioni continued. 'It was so different back then. It was taboo for pregnant women to be under the same roof as the chief, so I barely saw your father unless I was invited to eat with him. It was so lonely. As the chief's wife the other women were respectful when I went to market or the river, but I still missed him.'

'It must've been nice when Mosi was finally born and you

could live with Dad again?' Precious said to her mother.

Kioni smiled sadly, 'I wish. The day Mosi was born I fell in love with her immediately. I couldn't wait for everyone to meet her and love her just as much as I did. I was only sixteen, and I knew that some people would be disappointed that she was a girl, but I didn't care.

'One of your father's cousins came to visit me and told me Kidake had instructed him to get the beater and sound the drum to announce the birth of his son. When he saw it was a girl, he shook his head and walked away. Even my parents were disappointed, but they still loved me.'

Precious listened quietly. She knew life had been difficult for Kioni, being the wife of the chief and the mother of four daughters was never going to be easy, but she was only beginning to appreciate how much she'd suffered. She imagined what it would be like if she and Adrian had a child and he stopped speaking to her and blamed her if it turned out to be a girl. She'd be completely heartbroken.

Precious felt close to her mother; a deeper love than she had felt before. The intimacy was like a transplanted flower rediscovering its roots.

Chapter 9: Flight
Flying home? But where is home

The flight back to London felt different. The journey to Kenya had been awkward, wanting to tell Adrian things he needed to know and then suppressing them, not being open with him.

Now she was alone with her thoughts, Precious couldn't help looking at the present and allow herself to dream about the future. The engagement, the baby boy Kioni had adopted, the closeness to Nechesa. Now she was more of an equal rather than the big sister she had to look up to. It had happened at lightning speed and she felt as if she was catching up as a frisson of freedom lightened her body and mind. It was as if she had come out of survival mode.

The relief gripping her also filled her with guilt. She was leaving Tusanda and her African family behind. She was going to her new home and to her new life with Adrian. Surely Kioni had enough people around her to look after her? She had been surprised to read one of Kidake's letters when he talked about the need to get away and she thought,

'My father and I actually have things in common. He wanted to travel and study in the USA but had to give that up. But maybe he never quite lost the desire to be a free spirit.'

She had made a copy of his account of his flight to England to attend the coronation and took it out to read again.

"It was my first experience of flying. The journey took only three days, stopping overnight at Khartoum and Malta. The British Overseas Airway Corporation used a de Havilland Comet to fly from Johannesburg to London via Nairobi. It was like an idea of paradise, being waited on by beautiful women and served food and drinks throughout the flight. Once we arrived in London, I felt like I was in a dream. The city was

so impressive, exactly what you'd expect of the capital of the world's largest empire. I'd seen photographs and Pathé news clips of the city, but they were black and white. In June, the city doesn't have that grey aspect but is filled with colour. The gold and cream of the buildings, the red, white and blue profusion of flags everywhere one looked and the green of the many parks coloured those printed images. My favourite park is St James's. Close to the birds, water and fertile land, it felt more like home.

I spoke too soon about the weather—June 2nd was a drizzly day. It didn't stop the crowds turning out to watch the procession under thousands of umbrellas. Many people had camped out overnight in order to get a good view. I was in the Abbey so didn't see the procession but I read in the paper that the Queen of Tonga was particularly popular with the crowd. She refused to be under cover but let the rain wash over her.

The setting of this coronation in this great cathedral was so different to mine but there are similarities; the crowning and the sceptre and all the symbols of power. The music was beautiful but remote. I thought of the music at my coronation. It was celebratory but people could express themselves in dance. This coronation was a glorious performance to be witnessed .This experience has been a privilege, so why do I feel uneasy? Before coming to England, I knew who I was: Kidake, son of Katema and Aluna. I belonged to the fertile teeming land of the Tanga. In this city people stare at me. They don't see me as a leader or an individual. They look no further than the skin colour that marks me out as African."

Her father had communicated his love of London to her and that was why she was on this Airbus so unlike the little aircraft that had taken him to the Coronation.

She was jolted out of her trance by the pilot announcing they were approaching Heathrow, and her desire to be reunited with Adrian made London feel more like her home now. As they circled around Heathrow, she looked down at the streets, the lakes and the green landscape and felt a strong desire to belong to the country beneath her. She didn't want to feel as her father had that she would be defined by the colour of her skin. She wanted to belong.

This was no fantasy England. She knew it too well. She still felt scared by the murder of Abeo and she knew that the approaching trial would be traumatic and upsetting. She also knew that she would never be fond of the English winter, but then neither were the English. The difference was she knew another climate in her bones.

She smiled to herself as she pictured the kinder side to London, where people were conscientious and strove to make it a better place. The community at Crossroads and people like Darrel and Katie filled her with hope that London could be the place where her desire to run finally left her, and where she could dream of having a family who could thrive and excel. She felt reconciled with her father. She had not lost her resentment at his refusal to give her school fees but he had tried to make up for that by funding her degree. Reading his correspondence she had begun to understand him and believed that would help her put the past well and truly behind her. As she got off the plane she wanted to walk into her future.

'Welcome to London. The time is 05:30 AM and the temperature is fourteen degrees centigrade. Thank you for flying with us and we wish you a safe onward journey…'

Precious hurried to immigration and Adrian, anxious to hear about his dad. Her hopes of a quick exit were dashed when she saw the long queue in the line marked 'Non-EU passports'. Twenty-five minutes later she presented her Kenyan passport to the immigration officer. She peered over her glasses at Precious for what seemed like ages but was probably just a minute. It reminded her of her days in the head teacher's office so she attempted a smile but got no response. 'It's not her job to smile at passengers,' thought Precious.

She looked hard at the passport from cover to cover. Precious wondered what she could be looking for.

'I notice you came here on a student visa. You do realise that it's expired and I should have you deported?'

'But I've worked here ever since I was a student. Now I'm employed by the Metropolitan Police as a diversity trainer,' said Precious.

'In that case show me your police ID.'

She rummaged in her handbag. It was not there.

'I'm sorry I didn't take it with me to Kenya. I was going to my father's funeral. We left in a rush.'

'"We"? Who's "we"?' asked the immigration officer.

'My fiancé and I. We hope to get married soon.'

'And where is he?'

'He's British, but he's waiting at arrivals. He had to return early. His father was taken seriously ill,' said Precious.

The immigration officer looked straight at her. 'What did you say?

After Precious repeated herself, the immigration officer's cold eyes drilled through her.

'Have you notified the home office of your change of status?'

'What do you mean?'

'If, as you say, you work for the Met, you will know that you cannot just decide to get married without notifying the immigration office of your change in immigration status. According to my information you came here on a student visa.'

She asked her to sit down right in front of her desk on one of the chairs placed strategically in front of all the passengers. Precious, who had eagerly hurried from the plane, now sat there feeling humiliated. After a while the officer called her back. She asked more questions and yet again instructed her to sit in front of her desk. Passing passengers gave her strange looks, some of sorrow or pity, and others of disgust.

She was escorted to identify her luggage and forced to stand by as they methodically took it apart as if she was a drug dealer. They found nothing, but Precious was shown into a room and told to wait.

Another inspector entered and repeated the questions all over again. Precious was distraught.

'Please, telephone Inspector Ball. He will vouch for me.' She wrote down his number with nervous haste.

The officer left the room and returned fifteen minutes later.

'This isn't the number of Inspector Ball. Why do you keep lying?'

'I must have written it incorrectly. You have my bag. Please may I have my mobile phone? I can ring him and you can speak to him.'

Two-and-a-half hours after getting off the plane, Precious headed for the exit, worried that Adrian would be wondering why she hadn't appeared along with all the other passengers.

At first, she couldn't see him. She searched for him everywhere, and was just about to head for the tube station when she saw him sitting in a coffee bar. Rage, which she had carefully tamped down during the previous hours, flared.

'Why weren't you waiting for me? Couldn't you even do that for me?'

Adrian looked hurt. 'What do you mean, why couldn't I wait for you? I've been here for nearly three hours. I took the morning off work but that means I have to get back by two and work until eight.'

'So that's how things are! You go to work and I'll go to Katie's.'

'Aren't you going to tell me what happened?' Adrian asked. After the extended wait he was tired, confused and annoyed.

'I tried ringing your mobile. Take a look, there must be at least a dozen messages on it. Why didn't you answer?'

'Because I'm not welcome in this bloody country.'

Adrian's annoyance faded. It was the first time he'd heard Precious swear.

'Come on, let's head for the tube. Tell me about it on the way.'

On the tube she didn't feel like talking about it for the entire carriage to hear, so they sat in silence for the whole journey. Precious got out at Shepherd's Bush, but Adrian had to continue his journey to Wapping.

Once at the flat, she sat down and sobbed. She paced around the room, unpacked and then repacked her suitcase. She needed to talk to someone and the person who would listen was her friend Katie. Their first encounter was when Precious accompanied a victim of domestic violence to St Thomas' where Katie was a nurse. When they'd glimpsed each other at church, Precious went over to Katie and told her how much she admired the way she had handled the situation. Their friendship grew after that.

In need of her calm company, Precious rang Katie who picked up immediately.

'My shift has just ended. Do you want to come around for 2:30? It'll be lovely to catch up.'

Chapter 10: Things fall apart
Fallen leaves

As she walked towards her friend's flat, she slipped on some wet leaves. Her hand reached out for the trunk of the tree to stop herself falling, but the bark was slippery and she lost her grip and landed awkwardly on the cold pavement. Dejected, with stinging hands and knees, she climbed the stairs to the flat.

'Welcome back,' said Katie, smiling until she noticed Precious's glum face. 'Tea or something stronger?'

Suddenly, Precious felt ravenous. She hadn't eaten since the plastic meal on the plane nine hours ago.

'Can I order us a pizza? I'm feeling really hungry.'

The delivery boy was not long coming and Katie took some salad out of the fridge and opened a bottle of red wine.

'Here's to you and ... Adrian?' she toasted.

Precious looked as if she would burst into tears.

'Don't tell me you've broken up already?' Katie exclaimed.

Precious described what had happened. Regret flowed out of her with the force of the Victoria Falls.

'It wasn't his fault. I don't know why I turned on him like that, but I'm so confused Katie. When I left Nairobi, all I could think of was marrying Adrian. I had no doubts, but now I wonder whether I should go back to live in Kenya. If I'm not welcome, how can I make a home here?'

'Stop pacing around. Sit down and tell me about it properly. I'm a good listener. You have to be if you want to be a good nurse.'

Precious told her how close she felt to her mother after seeing her again.

'I'm worried about her. Will you believe it that at eighty she has adopted an abandoned baby?'

'But you have sisters in Kenya, Precious. Can't they help?'

'You're right, Katie. I'm finding excuses but immigration – that treatment has unsettled me. It makes me feel like I don't belong here. There have always been guys like Sergeant Jones who made it plain that he doesn't like black men, let alone black women in the force. But I thought his kind of prejudice was on the way out.'

Katie put her arms around Precious and gave her a sympathetic hug.

'I don't know why I shouted at Adrian but I wanted to provoke him. I think I was looking for any excuse to start an argument that would give me an excuse to break up with him without feeling guilty? Of course, you don't know. Adrian proposed to me in Nairobi. I wouldn't call it a romantic proposal. I accepted but I'm not sure that I found it convincing.'

'Precious. You're twenty-nine. Don't you want a family of your own? Adrian's a good man. He must be worried too. His father is on my ward and I don't think he has long to live. I expect we'll transfer him to a hospice next week.'

'Oh my Lord!' gasped Precious. 'What sort of a person am I? In my bitterness I didn't ask about George.'

'Why not ask now? Give him a ring,' suggested Katie.

She tried but Adrian's phone went to answer phone mode. She started to leave a message but it didn't come out right so she stopped mid-sentence.

'What a mess, Katie. What am I going to do?'

'You need some rest. Stay here tonight and go back to Shepherd's Bush in the morning.'

'I'm due at work tomorrow but my head is somewhere else. I feel utterly useless. You're right, Katie. The world may look different in the morning.'

The Met

'Welcome back, must've been a cold welcome after Kenya?' said Sergeant Johnson with a smirk. The news of the call to Inspector Ball had spread and he found it immensely satisfying that this haughty woman had got her comeuppance.

Precious ignored the sarcastic tone in his voice and tried to sound cheerful.

'It's good to be back, Sergeant. Although you didn't ask about my father's funeral. It was memorable and very impressive really.'

With that, she swept into her office. Looking through her diary, Precious saw that she had a trustees' meeting on the Wentworth Estate scheduled for 6.30pm.

'Oh damn. I won't get back to Shepherd's Bush before 10:00 but I can't get out of it,' thought Precious.

Adrian's flat in Shepherd's Bush.

Precious unlocked the door. Adrian was working on his laptop. He turned, expecting her to say something, maybe even start shouting again. Instead, she crossed over to Adrian without a word and hugged him. He felt the desperation in her body.

'Precious, what's the matter? Are you going to tell me?'

The past two days poured out of her.

'Adrian, will you forgive me? None of this is your fault. I didn't even have the grace to ask you about George.'

Adrian pulled away from the embrace and looked into her eyes.

'Of course, I forgive you. I can't imagine what it was like and I'm just sorry that I wasn't there to help you.'

Precious was filled with relief at his understanding and let him lead her to the bedroom. He helped take off her coat and stroked her tenderly until she dissolved in tears. She felt herself fall into his embrace. That night Precious learned that, following a row, reconciliation can be sweet.

Afterwards Adrian whispered, 'When I got back from the hospice seeing George looking helpless in that hospital bed I missed you until it hurt. I couldn't sleep and I didn't want to think about what happened when we met at the airport. I don't know what made me. I hadn't read poetry since I started work but I took out my copy of Keats. Do you know the poem he wrote when he was dying?'

Precious didn't know what to say so she just shook her head and said, 'Will you read it to me… please'

He reached out to the bedside table and it opened on that poem and he read her some extracts.

'When I have fears that I may cease to be

Before my pen has gleaned my teeming brain,'

Adrian paused looking with intense longing at Precious then continued,

'And when I feel, fair creature of an hour,

That I shall never look upon thee more

Of the wide world I stand alone, and think

Till love and fame to nothingness do sink.'

When he finished he turned to Precious and one of her tears dropped on his face.

'How can I have been so selfish, Ade? You were going through such grief and all I could think of was myself. I took my anger and hurt out on you. I'm so so very sorry.'

'Don't be sorry. You had too much to handle. Witnessing Abeo's murder and being threatened and then having to confront issues from your childhood. It's not surprising that the humiliating experience at immigration felt like a final straw. I've a suggestion to make. You told me about the Amah's suggestion for a trust. We didn't get a chance to discuss it. Maybe that could be a means of turning something dark into something positive. I know my girl and she's a positive force.'

Royal Trinity Hospice

This was Precious's first time visiting a hospice and she didn't know what to expect. She could hardly believe her eyes. The young woman on reception was dressed as a lit-up Christmas tree. With everything that had happened she had forgotten that it was December 8th and Advent had already begun. Chris, the social worker, showed them into his cosy office.

'We want you to know that we're here for you any time. George may even manage to get home for a while if we can get his medication right. The one thing we don't want is for him to suffer.' Chris's warm Australian accent was calm and soothing. 'Pain relief is the priority here. If we can get that right, George can go home. It's one of my roles, helping to make that possible. Is there someone who can be with him?'

'We could move him in, couldn't we Precious?' asked Adrian.

'Of course, but we both have demanding jobs. How do we arrange 24-hour care?'

'There's help we can put in place. The Macmillan nurses are wonderful. They will be a support for you as well as George. Think about it, and we can talk again later in the week.'

Chris led them to George's room. Delroy was sat next to his bed. George did the introductions.

'I've heard so much about you, Delroy. I'm so pleased to meet you again. Do you remember that we met on my first visit to George?'

Delroy nodded, 'Of course I do. Let me bring up a chair for you.'

'How're you feeling, Dad?' asked Adrian. 'Chris, who showed us here, says that you might be able to go home once they have the medication right.'

'Look Son, that'll be good, but there's no cure, is there? That's why I'm in here. I admit I felt dread at the word 'hospice', but I'm discovering that this is the place you come to live a bit longer with some quality of life.'

Delroy scoffed. 'You've never had it so good'. But he smiled at his friend.

'The social worker says that George could be at home but he couldn't really be in a better place, could you, my old friend? The staff can't do enough for you and we can visit any time, day or night.'

'Delroy here was reminding me of a prank we played on our local bobby when we were growing up in Notting Hill.' George said with a wink. 'With a policewoman here, we'd better be careful what we say from now on, Delroy.'

The change in George's tone gave them such relief that they were able to laugh, until George's laugh turned into a painful distressing cough. A nurse hurried in. She suggested they go to the garden room while she helped George.

They settled into the comfy chairs in the conservatory.

'George was telling me about you, Precious. He thinks it's about time Adrian had a partner,' said Delroy. Precious blushed, but she couldn't keep the smile off her face. Knowing George approved of her and wanted her to be with his son made her happy.

As they drove home Precious said, 'You know that joke about me working for the police? There was something about Delroy's laugh. It was as if he was trying to make light of something darker?'

'You're right. Not all police officers are like Darrel and Inspector Ball. One of his reggae mates, Smiley Culture, was killed during a police raid on his house. That wasn't in the nasty eighties—it only happened five years ago, so it still feels raw to him.

'Growing up in the eighties, I noticed the difference between how the police looked at me and how they looked at my black friends. All the black kids were stopped and searched without exception, and some were changed by the experience. I wouldn't have blamed them if they had resented me because I never got stopped, but any bad feeling between us was short lived. The world hasn't changed enough, has it?'

Precious sighed and looked introspective.

'It's not altogether a case of black and white. I remember a white boy in our street who went a bit AWOL after his father beat him. He threw a brick through the pub window where his dad had been drinking. He was soon in court and ended up with a criminal record.

'It's not a fair world is it? When certain members of our government were at Oxford, they joined the Bullingdon club, which regularly caused damage in pubs. They never ended up in court, or behind bars. They ended up ruling the country.'

'The privilege that comes with wealth and power is the same everywhere in the world,' said Precious. 'But you are right Ade. I don't want to be negative because that won't change anything.'

Despite the depressing turn of their conversation, she looked admiringly at Adrian, so at ease in London's multicultural society. He belonged. Precious yearned to belong. She remembered the horror at meeting her father's young wives at 'home'. She couldn't accept polygamy and felt estranged from her old life in Kenya. Her identity had been altered and now she thought British thoughts most of the time, but would she ever feel that England was her home?

She thought being black she would at least feel part of the black community like Delroy, but the memory of Abeo's young face in her arms kept surfacing. It reminded her that she was African and not all black Londoners welcomed her. Then there were white racists who would love her to return to Kenya. Could being with Adrian make this place her home? Would this Londoner's ease of belonging rub off on her, or was she too self-conscious to ever really belong here?

She looked at Adrian but he seemed lost in thoughts of his own. He had been strong while with George but Precious knew that he loved his dad deeply but probably wouldn't say so in those words.

She reached over and gave him a comforting squeeze of his hands. He smiled back and Precious saw his shoulders drop and felt him release a breath.

'What can I do to support you'? she asked.

'You're already doing everything right.' But he thought to himself, 'Keep it together or I'll be no use to George.'

Chapter 11: A Dilemma
To accept or not to accept

Joshua Amah rang asking Adrian and Precious to visit him and his wife. In the end, Precious had to go alone because Adrian was called to a press conference.

They showed her into an almost empty flat. They sat around the remaining dining table and Grace brought tea and biscuits.

'I'm sorry I didn't reply to the email. The signal was erratic and.. '

Joshua interrupted her and said, 'You can see that we have sold what we can. We plan to leave for Ghana after the trial. This can't be our home anymore.'

'I understand' said Precious. 'Losing a child…'

'But he wasn't lost, was he?' interrupted Grace. 'He was killed. We asked you here for two reasons. We wanted to thank you. We have faith that your testimony will bring Abeo the justice he deserves.'

'We're grateful,' said Joshua. 'You've done a lot for us, but can we ask you to do something more?'

Precious listened as they told her of their plans. They wanted her to ensure that Abeo's death would have a legacy and serve as a dire warning of the consequences of allowing the African and Afro-Caribbean communities to be estranged. They wanted to keep alive the memory of the happy, smiling boy who had ingratiated himself wherever he went, and to instil the hope that there could be reconciliation between the teenagers in the two communities.

Precious watched as Grace's face changed to one of steely conviction as Joshua spoke of the good they wanted to come from their tragedy. What else could Precious do but take her hands and promise her support?

On her way home she glimpsed Delroy buying cherries from a street vendor. She waved to him and crossed the road.

'Delroy, have you got time for a chat?'

'Anything for you, Precious.'

∞

She told Delroy about her promise to the Amahs.

'I can help you. I'm going to miss George. He's been a part of my life forever and I'll need something to focus on now I'm retired.'

They debated long and hard.

'The tension between some Afro-Caribbeans and Africans feels to me like the kind of prejudice I experienced as a young guy. Do you know how it put paid to my footballing career?'

Precious nodded. 'George told me.'

'I admire today's young black footballers. They experience all that crap. It's horrible here, but it can be even more vile and demeaning abroad. They have learned how not to lash out. How do they manage to restrain themselves? I lost my rag when opposition players mimicked the crowd's monkey chants. It's hard to explain how it affected me. I knew they wanted to demean me, make me lose my confidence, throw me off balance and to a point they succeeded.'

'How would you explain the divide between Afro-Caribbeans and Africans in London?' asked Precious.

'I don't really know the answer to that. Up to a point all immigrant groups are comfortable in their own communities. Our names and Caribbean culture is main stream in the UK. My son told me how an African boy in his school was teased to the point of bullying because his unpronounceable name set him apart. Some Africans make no secret of the fact that they think they are better educated and superior to us. I'm sure they are the exceptions but you've made me think about it.'

Precious was nodding when Adrian walked in.

'You two look serious.'

'I am serious for once, brother,' said Delroy.

Adrian raised an eyebrow in surprise.

'I know what you're thinking. You've never heard a good word about the police come out of my mouth, and here I am agreeing to collaborate with someone who works for them.'

Delroy looked at Precious and felt he owed her an explanation.

'When I hit thirteen if you had black skin hardly a month passed without either me or one of my black brothers being man-handled by the f… They called it 'Stop and Search'. Sure, they said there had been an incident in the area, but did they think that we didn't notice that they never stopped the white guys? When we reached the age to party, our parties were regularly broken up by the police. The middle-class types up in Hampstead with their cocaine-snorting gigs were never raided. The media, with some exceptions,' —he nodded towards Adrian— 'don't get it. They haven't had our experiences. When newspapers claimed that Mark Duggan shot at the police, even middle-class black friends and black MPs knew it was nonsense.'

Delroy sighed and smiled at Precious.

'I suppose it was inevitable that I'd start to mellow at sixty–five. Your mate Darrel is a good sort, and I'm surprised I can say that about anyone in his uniform. But I want my grandchildren to grow up without being afraid of the cops, so if I have to bite my tongue and do this I will.'

His tirade moved the chess pieces and created an opening.

'Pour us a glass of something and we can talk about what to do,' Delroy suggested.

Adrian did as he was told, but Precious looked concerned.

'I thought we'd be talking about how to raise money, but it's also about changing mind sets. That takes so much time and effort. My work with the police has been about trying to change perceptions, Delroy. I do know what you are talking about. Let's talk about the young people. What upsets me most is how tribal this feels. It could almost be in Kenya during the last elections when tribal allegiances led to conflict. A gang controls a given territory and if someone from outside that territory looks threatening, they attack. They see it as 'self-defence.' Do you think that the easiest way to get them to talk and to see things differently will be to take them out of the environment that reinforces those allegiances?'

'But to do that we'll need to raise money' said Adrian. 'The question is how? Looking thoughtful he added, 'This murder touched people's hearts. When the trial begins there'll be even more media attention. I'll ask my editor if I can include an appeal when I report on the trial. I'm sure loads of people will want to help.'

Precious makes a decision.

The London Post didn't hesitate. They not only agreed to publish information about the Abeo Amah appeal but to donate to it. The editor knew that not only was it an important cause but it could be good for the paper's profile and circulation. The board of trustees which included the great and the good, like the paper's principal share-holder, were to be joined by Adrian, Precious and Delroy at the request of Abeo's parents. The three of them met to come up with suggestions to put to the first meeting.

'Given your experience with Crossroads, you're the perfect person to run this, Precious,' said Adrian.

'I'm not sure Ade—I'm African. That's fine with the majority of people on the estate but not with the minority that the Amah's want us to work with. Me being African will be like a red rag to a bull.'

'This project is about connecting people; it's about

reconciliation.' said Delroy. 'I am Caribbean and you are African. We can to do this together.'

'Exactly!' said Adrian and he drafted a proposal.

Part 3:
London and Kenya

Chapter 1: The South Bank. December 2016
Life is full of surprises

Adrian knew that he was acting uncharacteristically, but these were tumultuous times and he had to be decisive. He owed it to George.

Precious was amused by the secrecy. Adrian wasn't one for surprises. They emerged from the tube at London Bridge at 4.00pm. It was the shortest day of the year, and the light was already fading as Adrian led her into the Shard and onto the lift to the restaurant. Precious gasped as she saw the view of the river, the London Eye, Tower Bridge and Westminster.

Adrian had booked them a champagne tea.

'I wanted to give you a special thank you for agreeing to come and live with George when he comes out of the hospice.'

'This is lovely, Ade, but there's nothing to thank me for. I like George and his friends. I wish I could do more.' The last sentence was almost a whisper.

The sky was darkening, but it was a cloudless night, and they wandered over to the huge windows just as the lights of London were at their theatrical best.

'It's magical,' sighed Precious.

'I'm glad you think so,' said Adrian, 'because I've something to ask you.'

Precious wondered if Adrian was preparing her for some bad news so she looked concerned.

Then he pulled something out of his pocket.

'I want to do this properly, Precious. You're the best thing that's ever happened to me. Everything got messed up didn't it? Do you still want to marry me?'

He took a diamond solitaire engagement ring out of an elegant box. Precious didn't know whether to laugh, cry or smile.

'I said 'yes' to the most unromantic proposal a girl ever had, so how can I refuse you now you've turned into quite the Romeo? Yes, Adrian let's do it!'

Adrian slipped the ring onto her outstretched hand.

'How did you get the right size?' asked an astonished Precious as it fitted perfectly.

I borrowed a ring from your jewellery box. I hadn't seen you wear it and didn't think you'd notice it going missing for a few hours.'

'You're full of surprises, Ade. Be careful, I might expect this all of the time.'

'I have made myself be decisive, Precious. I owe that much to George.'

He looked deep in thought then in a quiet voice said,

'Would you consider a quick wedding so that he can be present?'

'Of course, I'd love that.'

Adrian looked grateful.

'It's only when I faced losing both of you that I realised just how much I love you. Precious, I'm scared. George has always been there for me. He's never judged me and never tried to persuade me to do anything against my will.'

Precious felt lost for words. She kissed him and then looked sheepish, as she realised she'd kissed Adrian in a public place.

He smiled. 'Well, that was another first. We're doing quite well, aren't we?'

They laughed.

'If we arrange the wedding for March is there any chance your mother and sister could get here? What do you think?' asked Adrian.

Precious nodded her agreement through a smile that radiated the confidence of belonging.

Once back at the apartment Precious emailed Nechesa

and started to make plans for a March wedding. She prayed that Kioni could come and bless their marriage. It was thanks to her that it was possible. Kioni alone had valued her daughters and how had she returned that love? Her mother had suffered thanks to her running away. Kioni had forgiven her and understood—even supported—what she had done.

The experience of being in love and engaged to the man she wanted to spend the rest of her life with was overwhelming. Could the desire to flee, that had possessed her since she was a child, finally lose its hold?

∞

Being in Kenya had allowed Precious to escape from the memories of Abeo's death, but now she was back in London the trial loomed large. Every child she saw was a reminder of Abeo, and whenever she walked past the library she was overwhelmed by anxiety and sadness. Although the trial was not for months, the people at the Crown Prosecution Service were in constant contact with her, and the high-profile nature of Abeo's murder meant that they were using all their resources to achieve a conviction. After many emails back and forth, they wanted to go through her witness statement with her, and she knew that reading through the account would bring back the terrible memories of the small boy lying in her arms.

The meeting was as awful as she had imagined. The solicitor emphasised that her evidence would be challenged and the attempt would be made to make her look like an unreliable witness. She felt angry that someone would try and twist the truth so that a guilty person could walk free. Although everyone had the right to a fair trial, she felt that there would be no justice for Abeo if the defence was able to manipulate the evidence and the jury to their will. She was so preoccupied, as she left the building that she walked straight into a tall black guy.

'I'm so sorry. I wasn't looking where I was going.'

The man thrust what she thought was a flier into her free hand and hurried away without saying anything. She put it in her pocket without a second thought, and headed for the Underground.

Once on the tube, she realised it was an envelope. Curiosity got the better of her, and she ripped it open and pulled out a letter. As she read the message, she felt sick. 'We know who you are talking to. If you value your good looks, forget it.'

She was hardly through the door of their flat before Precious tore up the note. Although she thought about the trial often, her imminent wedding had given her a sense of safety and security, which had made her feel invincible. This second encounter with the Wolf Crew made her realise that this was more than intimidation. She looked at the pieces of paper and sighed knowing how silly it had been to rip up the note. She should have given it to Inspector Ball. She swept the pieces into an envelope and put them in a drawer in her desk. There was no mention of Nelson and Jacob, but there was no doubt in her mind that it was about the trial.

∞

After her father's funeral, Precious had started jotting down her thoughts. She wasn't sure where the urge had come from but acknowledged that her father's letters had affected her. They had helped her understand him and forgive him but not allowed her to forget the injustice she felt on behalf of the women in Tusanda. Now she wanted to write a new chapter in her life: a time in which she deserved to be loved and to love back, a life and place where colour was not a barrier, and she was valued for herself and not for her 'bride price' or Ikhwe. Was she writing an impossible dream? She had tried to put the past behind her and she wanted to ignore the threats too. She longed for hope and happiness. Was that so wrong?

Despite her resolution her thoughts kept returning to Tusanda and her mother. Had she received the invitation? Why had she sent Kioni a snail mail one? Yes, it was beautiful but she should have told Nechesa in her email to ring her.

Over supper, Adrian asked,

'What would happen if I had proposed in Kenya?'

'Well, your family would send a wanjira, a go-between, to verify that I am a hard-working girl from a reputable family. A spy would hide in the bushes for weeks, watching my every move to report back.'

'I can't see George doing that, can you?' laughed Adrian.

As she climbed into bed that night, she knew that she was being watched, but not by George. She felt the Wolf Crew's eyes on her through the windows. Should she believe the threats? No, she wanted to forget them, but then they kept churning in her mind so that she found it difficult to sleep.

'What's the matter?' asked Adrian in a tired voice.

Precious knew she should tell him, but she didn't want to break the spell of contentment she felt lying next to him. She reassured herself that she wasn't in serious danger. She told herself that they wouldn't risk an assault on someone who worked for the police. They were not that stupid. They wanted her to feel threatened but they wouldn't actually hurt her.

She tried counting cows and goats. But that only reminded her of Uncle Moses and his brothers agreeing her bride price. It would be thirteen to twenty heads of cattle, or the equivalent of a cow was four goats. A bull, three goats and sheep would be an insult. Instead she counted sticks. 'Counting the sticks' had a special meaning in Kenya. She visualised Adrian delivering a short stick with every animal.

She saw it being cut, marked and tied in a bundle with sticks denoting earlier instalments. If the marriage didn't work out and ended in divorce then some of the items would have to be refunded.

She must have fallen asleep, and when she woke in darkness she wasn't sure where she was. She looked at the grey shapes of the flowers and grasses in the vase on the table and smiled.

'I don't have to worry about Tusanda where marriage is arranged and the bride and groom have no say. I'm all human and not an asset with a price tag attached!'

She tried dozing off again. Her body was half asleep but her mind was active. Uncle Moses's words, 'stick to your own', kept ringing in her head as the bundles of sticks in her mind piled higher and higher and threatened to bury her.

The timer on her mobile phone went off. Precious had spent the whole night drifting in and out of sleep. In a state of half consciousness, she had suppressed thoughts about Nelson and the note and instead had pictured Adrian going through the traditions of Tanga culture.

She sighed. His only experience of Kenya was a funeral, and he hadn't understood half of what was being done, let alone said. To him, most of the activities had no meaning, but if they had to have a Luhiya wedding as well as a British one, it would be elaborate and accompanied by lots of singing, dancing, wedding photos and celebrations. The Luhiya love chicken and provided them in plenty for wedding guests. Adrian had recently become a vegetarian so she wondered how he would take all of that?

She didn't want to leave early, so she got ready for her meeting with Inspector Ball slowly. Before leaving the flat, she took out the envelope from the drawer and then put it back, slamming the drawer shut as if that was a problem solved.

Chapter 2: Kioni in London
Crossing continents

Kioni opened the neatly hand-written letter which enclosed Precious's wedding invitation and couldn't stop smiling. Her last-born daughter had finally found love and decided to get married. After the funeral, tongues had wagged. She hadn't been surprised. When an educated girl of a certain age is not married or pursued by a suitor from a reputable family, rumours spread.

'There has to be a reason that such a woman is not married.' They had gossiped.

Precious was known as the bride who had rebelled against tradition and moved out of the village, disrespecting the family and—even worse—the clan's culture.

'The curse of an unmarried aunt has befallen her as the black sheep of the family.' They whispered and so it went from mouth to mouth. It was even rumoured that she could be *Ishira* and that's why she might never get married. Some of the men had heard of a movement called *feminism* which had started somewhere in the West. Stories of women marrying other women were rife. Kioni heard someone joke that Precious might be one of those strange women.

In neighbouring Uganda women and men guilty of 'carnal knowledge against the order of nature' were being threatened with the death penalty. The Uganda Anti-Homosexuality Act, 2014 was passed on 17 December 2013 with a punishment of life in prison for 'aggravated homosexuality'. Kioni knew that some of the gay people who had fled their country sought refuge in a town close to Tusanda. But the gossips concluded that Precious probably wasn't one of them. Hadn't she been accompanied by Adrian, a white man?

Nechesa was the sister Precious had always turned to, so

Kioni rang her in Uganda to tell her the news and asked her to accompany her to London.

'I'd love to go. The girls are old enough to be left alone and I'm due a sabbatical. It won't be a paid one, but I'm lucky that Otieno is so supportive. We can't turn down this opportunity to travel outside of Africa.'

Kioni and Nechesa set to work to obtain all the paper work, health checks, and bank checks which were part of the visa requirements. Meanwhile in London Precious worked hard to ensure that her mother didn't encounter the problems that she'd experienced at immigration. The incident still felt raw, and Kioni wouldn't be able to cope with an interrogation, especially with the language barrier.

Kioni felt nervous of flying such a long distance and worried about what she would eat in England. Would she get her favourite *ugali*, a Kenyan staple food, and vegetable meal in London?

'Should we pack some food just in case?'

Nechesa reassured her and promised that once they got to London, Precious would make sure she was looked after.

∞

Precious took time off work to meet them at the airport. She'd booked them into a hotel overlooking the Thames. Precious felt this was her opportunity to show her mother and sister her love and gratitude for their support. She wanted to make this trip special and for them to have an amazing experience and not just at the wedding.

When she led them into their hotel room Nechesa gasped with excitement.

'Look at the size of this bed, Ma!' She stroked the white bed linen. She'd never seen anything so white.

'They must wash them with sparkling pure water not like the brown water from the Akwera,' said Kioni.

Nechesa turned to Precious.

'Do you remember when we were children how we used to go to the river to wash and after a good scrub we sat on the rocks beside the river to dry ourselves in the sun? We never had towels and the boys hid in the bushes to peep at us. I'd dress superfast and chase them away.'

Precious laughed at the memory but it was another thing she didn't miss about Tusanda. Later, she suggested they went out to find something to eat.

'I love my bed,' said Nechesa. 'I am not leaving my room. This bed is the most comfortable, cleanest bed I have ever seen. Why leave it to walk in the wind?'

Kioni was quiet. On the way, she had complained of how cold she felt. The wedding was set for three weeks' time, March 15. Spring was on its way, but Kioni was suffering even though it was relatively mild at ten degrees. The following day they relaxed in the hotel during the day, but Precious arranged to finish work early so that her special guests could help her choose her wedding dress.

She arrived at the hotel with thick padded coats, gloves, scarves and hats. They laughed when they saw themselves dressed for winter and took photos to send to friends and family in Kenya. The trio set out for the West End. Nechesa kept stopping every few minutes. Passing a restaurant, she was mesmerised by the size and type of bread.

'It's Italian and called pizza,' explained Precious. 'You must try it.'

Impressed, Kioni said, 'The cooks must be specialised. I wonder how many days it takes them to cook this special bread? Where can we can buy cassava?'

'I'm sorry, Ma, but we can't buy your favourite roast sweetcorn or fried cassava or even boiled maize like we do along the roadside from Tusanda to Bukora, but I'll cook them for you one day,' promised Precious.

'What do people from Africa who live here do when they have a craving for our homely foods?' asked Kioni. Before Precious could answer, Kioni and Nechesa's attention was distracted. They saw a man who looked distinctly African with a brush and bin collecting and sweeping up the rubbish. Precious read their thoughts.

'Are cleaning jobs only for black people, and why would he leave his beautiful African village to come here in the cold to clean the streets? Is he educated? What language does he speak? Maybe next time I see him I could 'Jambo' him (hello) in Kiswahili.'

Precious saw Nechesa and Kioni struggling with this new culture. In Tusanda it is considered rude to walk past someone and not say 'hallo' and find out about them and their village.

Nechesa looked back to see him scraping sticky chewing gum from the pavement and mused, 'Gum is so expensive why would anyone leave any stuck on the ground?'

They arrived at Selfridges and headed for the wedding dresses, which were on the second floor. Precious led them to the escalator and without thinking strode onto it leaving behind a nervous Kioni and Nechesa. They looked on as she rose swanlike further and further away from them.

Realising what had happened she called down to them.

'Stay there! I'll come back down for you.'

Once back down, she explained what they should do. After they watched other people for a few minutes, Precious guided her mother onto the first rung and held her hand all the way up. Once at the top, Kioni grinned but her smile disappeared when she saw the price of the dresses. Kioni took Precious to one side.

'Show me which one you like. Let's buy material in the market and I'll make it for you. We can make a beautiful wedding dress for a tenth of the price of what I have just seen. Do you not agree with me, Nechesa? Let us make it for you.'

'Oh Ma, that's lovely, but we don't have time and I don't want you to work,' said Precious who decided that it might be best to get Katie to help her choose the dress. But the cake was definitely her mother's area of expertise.

'Let's call it a day and go and enjoy a pizza. Tomorrow I'll take you to Brixton Market to a shop that makes cakes, and you can help me chose my cake.'

Brixton Market proved a success so after the disappointing previous day Precious let out a sigh of relief. They loved the choice of food and the vibrant atmosphere. They felt so at home that Precious was able to persuade them to let Delroy show them some of London's sights the next day while she worked. They also bought vegetables to cook one evening when they would eat at Adrian's place.

Adrian was nervous as well as excited to be entertaining his future mother-in-law. He wanted her to meet George so that they could get to know each other before the wedding, but he wondered how she would feel about going to the hospice.

Delroy arrived with Precious's mother and sister, carrying a Caribbean goat curry. Precious had made ugali to please her mother.

She and Adrian relaxed when they saw Kioni's beaming smile.

'This kind man took us to Westminster Abbey where your father attended the coronation of Queen Elizabeth II and then on a taxi ride to see Buckingham Palace. I never thought his wife, a poorly educated daughter of a pastor, would stand at the gates of that palace. Look! Delroy took a photo of us.'

After they admired the pictures on Delroy's phone Nechesa said, 'It's a shame the British abolished our ancestors' kingdom.'

'We have had a wonderful day, but now I'm tired,' said Kioni, ignoring her daughter's aside.

She perked up when she tried the food. When the salad came around a look of confusion crossed her face and she turned to Precious.

'Does your man not have money to buy oil to fry that vegetable?' she said in Luhyia. 'You didn't tell me he was that poor, even your uncle's sweeper Makokha gives his wife money to buy oil for the vegetables.'

Nechesa, who was the person other than Precious who'd understood, burst out laughing.

'Ma, that's called salad. Fresh leaves are eaten like that. It's not meant to be cooked,' said Precious and then in English, 'How do you like Delroy's Jamaican curry?'

Kioni nodded her approval.

'We Jamaicans know something about spice and flavour,' said Delroy, smiling. 'How much of that came from Africa? I don't know. So, how about you cooking some of your dishes?'

'We can't do that in the hotel' said Nechesa.

'No' said Adrian 'but I have a suggestion to make. Would you consider moving into George's house? We hope that after the wedding we'll move in too so that he has someone to look after him at home. We'll need to arrange for his care while we're at work, but the social worker at the hospice will help organise that. Alterations are being made to the bathroom as we speak.'

Nechesa and Kioni loved the idea and they wanted to help. They offered to clean the house and get it ready. They also wanted to meet George.

'There are no hospices in West Kenya so this will be a new experience for you. Don't worry, it's a welcoming place. Will you come with us tomorrow evening?' asked Precious.

Delroy arranged to pick them up the next day and take

them to the Notting Hill house. Precious gave him the money to settle the hotel bill. As they were going to see George the next day, she suggested they eat out in Notting Hill afterwards and Kioni and Nechesa could cook for them on Friday night.

The Hospice

At first, Kioni and Nechesa seemed reserved and ill at ease but then Delroy arrived. His easy-going manner settled their nerves and his questions about the wedding gave them something to focus on.

'We've chosen the cake,' Nechesa said excitedly, 'and the lovely thing is the sugar bride and groom on the top will look like Adrian and Precious. The bride is not white!'

George stroked Precious's hand.

'No. This lass is not in the least bit pale—she glows. I don't want to miss this wedding.' He waved to the nurse and said, 'You'll keep me going until the fifteenth March, won't you?'

The nurse reassured him.

'You'll be there, George. We've arranged for a palliative care nurse to accompany you. They won't need to fetch you. We'll arrange hospital transport. You'll be comfortable, I promise.'

Impressed by the nurse's kindness, tears welled up in Kioni's eyes.

For the first time Kioni spoke, 'Thank you. A wedding wouldn't be right without the father of the groom present.'

She felt a warmth and empathy for George and grasped his hands and squeezed them. 'I am so glad.' She turned to the nurse and repeated, 'Thank you, thank you.'

Later that evening over their meal, Kioni said to Precious, 'We need nurses like her in Tusanda. We need a health centre with good standards like I have seen today. If I had not taken in my baby son, Joseph, he would have died. After the wedding I want to talk to you about it.'

Chapter 3: The Wedding March 2017
Beginnings and endings

Adrian never expected this day would happen. He'd always run away from commitment, and he'd never much liked being the centre of attention. But for Precious and George, he felt he could manage even that. Some of his old university friends would be amused by the inexpensive wedding. A few worked in academia, but others had gone into the city and made money. He didn't envy them. He had a life he loved.

Kioni was nervous as she put on the big beige hat her daughters had helped pick at Brixton market; she'd never worn a hat in her whole life. In Tusanda, hats were reserved for men of status. She looked in the mirror and felt important. Nechesa handed her a pair of cream gloves.

She put them on and stretched out her hands. They looked like the gloves the white colonial women had worn when they visited Tusanda with their husbands.

It had been whispered that they wore gloves because they didn't like touching black skin, but Kioni had dismissed that. She had admired their elegance. But the hat made her think of her husband. How would he have reacted to this wedding?

'No dowry has been paid and Precious is marrying a white man in a foreign country. What would he wear? His traditional regalia over a well-tailored suit like he wore at the Coronation?' Her mind never stopped until Nechesa said,

'Ma, are we not going to pray before we leave?'

A lot of Precious's friends attended the Pentecostal Church, so that was their chosen venue. Stylish? Definitely not. But it was warm, welcoming and inclusive in spades. The congregation which waited for the bride and groom to arrive were from Crossroads, the Met and African friends of Precious. George and Adrian had invited their Afro-

Caribbean friends as well as journalists and his mates from university. Even old school friends like Jaysee turned up. Katie and Nechesa were Precious's bridesmaids, and Kioni was delighted to walk her down the aisle. The Gospel Choir who sang at Abeo's memorial service raised their voices and set a mood of genuine celebration.

After the ceremony, Precious worried that they might have made a mistake when choosing the reception venue: the refurbished community centre on the Wentworth estate. They wanted it to exorcise the dark mood that had engulfed it since Abeo's death.

The residents came out in force to cheer them. Delroy and DJ Euton had been introduced and had together arranged the entertainment. They clicked like old friends despite crossing generations. Icolyn was in charge of the catering. Adrian had made a generous payment so she could cover costs, pay herself and the helpers and still have a large donation for the soup kitchen.

When Adrian and Precious walked through the door, it blew their mind. Precious began to cry tears of joy.

'Who did this?' she asked as she saw the hall festooned with African flowers and African fabrics draped on the wall. Euton's disco's lights created starlight like the wonderful African night sky. Everyone was dressed in the bright colours of Kenya and the Caribbean.

Precious in her elegant white wedding dress stood out and felt as if she had arrived in the wrong continent. Kioni beamed and sat next to George. They held hands like an old married couple. Precious and Adrian went around the room speaking to everyone.

Katie whispered in Precious's ear, 'You look stunning but even better – you look happy.'

Precious glowed with appreciation and took her aside,

'I am happy Katie. It was only three months ago when

I stopped overnight with you - I couldn't have believed it possible.'

Adrian waved to Jaysee and left the girls talking.

'Do you remember the story I told you about when I was sixteen and my parents were away and I had to look after some visiting relatives?'

'Remind me' said Katie.

'It was late one evening after a long and hard day. When I refused to iron an aunt's dress, she was angry with me and said, "I can't believe how your mum has spoilt you. Do you think you are too important to do the ironing? Have you looked at yourself lately in a mirror? Do you know how ugly you are? Of all your father's children you are the ugliest. Get out of here you make me sick just looking at you." Because of that I never thought a man could ever love me. You taught me to believe that someone as tall and muscular as me can still be beautiful. Thank you so much for being my bridesmaid– for sharing this day Katie.'

'It was a pleasure– a delight. You deserve happiness. Grab it while you have it.'

So much love had gone into the food preparation that guests talked about it for weeks afterwards. Once every one had eaten, some of the tables were put away, and the rhythms of the Caribbean and of Africa enticed the guests. Adrian came over and confidently took her hand.

'Everyone wants to dance, but they insist we must dance first.'

The mixture of music and dance was so communal that soon almost everyone was on their feet having a good time.

As the volume increased the palliative care nurse who had accompanied George was concerned. 'We must decide on a time to leave.'

A flicker of relief crossed George's face.

'It's been a great day. Thank you for sharing it with me

and helping me, but you're right. I'll be fine for maybe thirty minutes more but yes please, I'd like to go back to Trinity.'

Half an hour later, an emotional Adrian and Precious saw George into the hospice transport. He was insistent that they return to their guests, but they waited until the ambulance left.

'My darling girl, thank you. It would've been a more sophisticated wedding if we'd waited, but it means so much to me and George that he could be here today,' said Adrian.

'It feels not quite right being happy while Dad is dying but I know it is right because he loved the wedding. You can see it meant a lot to him. Everyone he cared about is here. You do realise that all these people celebrating with us were also saying good bye to him.'

Adrian choked back tears.

'That's the first time I've called George 'Dad' in ages.'

Precious held him close and said,

'I love your father, Ade. I wish I had longer to get to know him. After the weekend we'll bring him home—I promise. My mother likes him too. You've seen that for yourself. She'll stay on and help.'

As they walked back into the hall, Darrel took them aside.

'I didn't want you to hear this on the news. The date has been set for the trial of Nelson and Jacob. Its two months from now at Oxford Crown Court. They don't want it on their doorstep. I expect you'll be hearing from the Crown Prosecution next week.'

'Thank you, Darrel. I hope they change their minds and plead guilty. That could save Joshua and Grace Omah a lot of anxiety and it would be great not to be a witness.'

No Honeymoon

Adrian and Precious spent two nights in a hotel not far away in Richmond and they tried not to think of George, Abeo,

Nelson or Jacob. After brunch, they walked in Richmond Park. Looking at the deer grazing in a group among the trees, Adrian said,

'It's not exactly a sand, sea and sunshine Facebook honeymoon but at least there's some wildlife.'

'It's perfect. We'll have lots of opportunities for holidays but not much time left to enjoy George's company. The Met has been supportive considering the time I had off for my father's funeral. I'll have to make up this week at some point and looking after George is not how they expected me to spend it, but that's what we both want, isn't it?' said Precious.

'He's got the MacMillan nurses, Kioni, Nechesa, you and me. We'll show him how much he's loved. Their tourist visa is for three months, but I need to talk to my mother about a few responsibilities she's left behind in Kenya.'

Chapter 4: George comes home
Trust a bunch of women

In the space of just over a year, Adrian's life had gone from being solely about him and his work, to being filled full of people. This was different from friends. This was definitely family, and he sensed that it was only the beginning.

Adrian and Precious rearranged the furniture so that George didn't need to go upstairs. Nechesa painted the living room white and brought down all the most colourful paintings she could find around the house to hang them on the walls. The effect was both restful and cheerful. There was a bathroom on the ground floor and only minor adjustments had been needed. When George was wheeled through the door, he looked around in surprise.

'Trust a bunch of women. You turn your back for one second and they've organised your whole life. I'll never find my stuff now.' He seemed serious, and Nechesa looked upset until little lines appeared at the corner of George's mouth, and he broke out into a rare smile.

'I love it. Thank you.'

Adrian put on a vinyl record—Reggae—just as Delroy walked in and began to sing to the strains of Bob Marley.

'Now that reminds me of our trip to Jamaica when you kind of retired.'

Adrian noticed George smile. It was a weak smile now but only Delroy seemed able to achieve that.

A palliative care nurse called every day and could be rung at any time. It was such a relief to Adrian and Precious that when they left for work, they knew George would not be alone Nechesa and Kioni were there, and often when Adrian returned from work and turned the key he entered to the sound of laughter.

'Are you going to share the joke?' he asked.

Precious looked at Nechesa. Her sister drew herself up tall and straight, lifted George's stick and banged it hard on the floor, pretending to be Uncle Moses.

'You need to respect your elders, Precious Lutta. Shut up and listen to your father-in-law.'

'I want to meet this Uncle Moses,' said George, while the women laughed. 'Sounds like British guys could learn a thing or two from him,' and he winked at Adrian. Speech was becoming more difficult for him but George had not lost his sense of humour.

Adrian stared at George. Nechesa had painted some strange lines on his face. Seeing his glance, she said,

'We've been dancing – not like you do here. George joined in from his chair.'

'Are you going to demonstrate it to me?' asked Adrian.

'There's a Tanga traditional dance that involves shaking your backside. It's rarely performed nowadays. George enjoyed it but, no way am I going to show you Adrian! Let's eat.'

As they cleared away the dishes a worried expression crossed Precious's face.

'What is it, Precious?' asked George.

'You have more than enough to cope with George, you don't want to listen to my worries.'

'Now there you're wrong. I know I haven't long, but in the time I have left, I want to be part of life. If I share your experiences, I'll live longer Precious.'

'Joseph and Nelson have pleaded 'Not Guilty'. I have to testify and I have a few concerns but I don't want to think about them. But thank you George.'

∞

Two weeks later, George's breathing became so gruelling that he needed to be on oxygen twenty-four hours a day. Caring for him became difficult and George suggested he spend his last weeks in the hospice.

'There's no use pretending. I'm not going to get any better. Thank you for …' The sentence was interrupted by a coughing fit that sounded as painful as it felt. Nechesa plumped up his cushions and Precious called the nurse.

The final days

George asked Adrian to visit on his own.

'I need… to talk to you, son, while I can.'

Adrian could see how his father was struggling to get the words out and waited patiently.

'During the last month I've got to know Kioni.'

Adrian nodded.

'I see where Precious gets her strength from.'

After a minute George tried again.

'Kioni told me about the baby she adopted. The village is struggling to cope with the orphans. She has an idea.'

George took a long draft of oxygen.

'A Day Centre could support the extended families and make all the difference.'

Adrian held a glass of water to his father's lips. George took a sip and continued.

'You'll inherit everything—well, not quite everything—Delroy'll get my record collection and I'll leave the money in my bank account to the Carnival.'

Adrian was not a man to show his emotion, but he struggled to hold back tears. George patted his hand and seemed to have some respite as he said,

'When your grandfather moved to Notting Hill it was regarded as the pits, and now it's a millionaire's paradise. Use some of the money from the house to help her. I'll say as much in the will, but I won't stipulate how much. I know you and Precious will find a way.'

Two weeks later George died with all the family and Delroy by his bedside.

Chapter 5: Past, present and future
The son I never had

George's death wasn't unexpected and his father had looked so peaceful in his last moments. The shock Adrian experienced surprised him. Then he felt the loving embrace of three women. How different this moment would have been without them.

He hadn't realised how much people in the area loved his dad. Why not? Notes and cards were dropped through the letter box some telling stories he didn't know. People of all colours were visibly moved and when he was walking to the tube men and women – he had no idea who they were – stopped him or crossed the road to give their condolences. Despite his journalist training he often forgot to ask who they were and their connection to his father. Why hadn't he asked his father more questions when he could?

Precious arranged to meet Kate and some old friends after work. They had booked a table for dinner in a restaurant not far from her old flat. After the women's hostel, this had been her first proper home in London. Even though she didn't own it, it had felt like her own place. It was some kind of sentiment that prompted her to make a short detour to pass it. As she turned the corner, she heard a crack of glass. A man rather like the one who had thrust the note in her hand was running away.

When she reached the flats, she saw that the window of her old flat was smashed. Taped to the door was another threatening note.

Precious rang Inspector Ball and told him what had happened. He told her to wait there, and he would send a car. While she waited, she called her friends. She didn't want to alarm them so she just apologised.

'I was on my way, but I've just had a call from work, and I have to go back to the station. I'm so sorry. What with George dying, I really needed cheering up.'

∞

'You know you've been an idiot, don't you Precious? The good news is they don't realise that you're living in Notting Hill, but that could change. You have to take these people seriously.'

Precious bit her lip. She didn't take kindly to being called an idiot. She was, after all, a police trainer. It didn't do anything for her self-esteem. She knew Inspector Ball was just concerned for her welfare, and she reluctantly admitted to herself that he was probably right.

'You must bring that note into the station in the morning and no more secrets. It's evidence.'

Having been brought up in West Kenya close to the border with Uganda, Precious knew about the barbarities wrought by evil men who cared only for power. She'd met refugees from Idi Amin and the brutal Lord's Resistance Army. But this was London and she had denied the danger.

She walked fast, and then ran as if speed alone could make her safe. She wondered what she should tell Adrian. She took a deep breath and decided she'd tell him the same story she had told her friends. He had enough on his plate arranging the funeral. There would be time enough after that.

The Funeral

'I don't know how I'd have coped without you and your family, Precious. George was all I had. You made those final weeks special for him. I could never have done that.' Precious smiled and gripped Adrian's hand.

'How's the planning going? Did you get the music sorted?'

'Oh, don't worry. George talked to Delroy about all the

music before he died.'

'He wants none of your dirges Adrian,' Delroy teased. 'I'll see to that while you let people know about the funeral.'

Precious knew that George wasn't religious, but she suggested to Delroy that they involve the Gospel Choir.

'It could help many of the mourners, and he didn't dislike their passionate singing, did he?'

In the end they decided to have a memorial for George in the local church hall. Only the close family would go with the body to the crematorium. Kioni was relieved. She didn't understand why a son would want to burn his father's body and asked not to go.

The memorial could not have been more different to the ceremonies in Tusanda. It lasted two hours because all his musical friends wanted to pay their respects to him with the sounds he had loved. There had been order to begin with, but after a while the assembly took on a Quaker element. Adrian was so moved by the number of people who wanted to stand up and say something about his father. They described practical help he had given them and others talked about how George had provided a sympathetic ear and a touch of humour at the right time.

That evening Kioni said, 'Precious, Nechesa, when I go, I'd like something like that.' They held their mother tightly.

'You're not going anywhere yet, except home to Tusanda.'

Precious booked Kioni and Nechesa's return tickets for the following week. During those last days in London, Nechesa spent a lot of time in the British Library and British Museum and enjoyed talking about her discoveries with Adrian.

She described an Egyptian sculpture.

'I'd swear he was black. Why was his nose knocked off? Do you think there is some denial going on here? Our father told us that our people originally came from Egypt. I thought it was just myth and story- telling. But could there be truth in it?

Adrian was worried.

'Precious how are we going to fulfil George's will. We haven't told your mother about his wishes. We have to do that before she leaves.'

'I've so enjoyed having them here that I haven't really thought it through. What are we going to do Ade?'

∞

The night before their flight to Kenya they talked about George's wishes. Kioni was surprised and moved by George's will. It came like a shock that numbed her brain. Eventually she whispered,

'What a good man. My life is richer for having known him, Adrian and you take after him.'

Adrian looked moved and said,

'We have a dream, but there is a lot of work to do to make it reality. Precious and I have been trying to come up with a plan. If we let my Shepherd's Bush flat, that will bring in a reasonable income. We need to explore the possibility of raising a mortgage on this house. Then we can convert it into three flats.'

Precious interrupted,

'We'll need capital from the house to finance the project. The planning and the work could take eighteen months. So, don't get excited yet.'

'The aim is to make the largest flat for Precious and me. We'll keep the smallest to let and the third to sell. The money from that sale will build the Day Centre.'

'I have to set up a charity to avoid tax on the sale so that all the money can be transferred to Tusanda,' said Adrian.

'We are still working out how to do the work involved. One idea is that I reduce my working hours so that I have the time to organise everything. The income from Adrian's flat should make that do-able', said Precious.

Kioni looked amazed.

'My son,' she said. 'You're the son I never had.'

Chapter 6: A Warning
Delroy is watchful

Precious was missing her mother and sister: their company had freed her mind from disturbing thoughts. The void after they left meant she beamed with pleasure when she bumped into Delroy as she walked down Kingsdown Road. Precious found that hard because she couldn't pass the spot where Abeo had been killed without that day being resurrected. Delroy noticed her unease.

'His killers will end up where they deserve to be – behind …'

He stopped mid–sentence as a car pulled up sharply beside them. The passenger window was open and a man with a black and white scarf covering most of his face leaned out.

'Precious. Watch out,' shouted Delroy and reached out to push her head downwards.

The alarm in his voice led to an instinctive reaction – a reaction that saved her. The man shouted in a South London accent as he threw the contents of a bottle at her.

'This is for Nelson.'

Precious screamed and Delroy turned but not before he tried to memorise the car number plate as it sped off.

The pain in her hands was excruciating but they had saved her face. Precious looked in horror as the skin peeled off leaving a bloody mess. Delroy pulled out a bottle of water from his bag and poured it over her hands. While he attended to her he asked a woman to call the police and an ambulance .

While waiting for an ambulance to arrive, Delroy asked everyone passing by for water and kept pouring it over Precious's hands. The paramedics were impressed.

'You did the right thing, mate.'

With gloved hands one bent down and picked up the bottle. This will help us identify the chemical. In the ambulance the paramedics continued to cool the burns and gave Precious strong pain killers. It had all happened so suddenly they worried that she could go into a severe shock. They made her drink and tried to get her to talk while reassuring her.

'Your friend acted so promptly that your hands could heal within weeks.'

Delroy called Adrian and he met them at the hospital in A&E where she was treated with antibiotic cream and painkillers while the bottle was examined. Precious and Adrian were impressed by Delroy. Not only had he acted to limit the damage to Precious's hands, but when the police interviewed him he'd remembered part of the number plate.

'It was a silver Toyota but I didn't catch the model. The guy didn't get out of the car. It sped away in seconds. I tried to read the number plate before it turned left down Canal Street. I'm pretty sure it began with GA and ended with an X. The numbers in the middle may have been 21, but I couldn't swear on it.'

Precious had not been wrong in thinking that the police would react vigorously when one of their own was attacked. Delroy's quick thinking helped them locate the car swiftly. It had been stolen and abandoned but they found a good CCTV image of the car and its driver and the culprits were soon under arrest. The chance of prosecution looked good as a little of the acid had dropped on the car door.

∞

Precious was allowed home two days later - her hands in bandages

'You'll need treatment every day to prevent infection. They should heal naturally and without the need of grafts.

Your friend and the paramedics did everything right so we have been able to minimise the damage. There will be permanent scarring but you should regain full use of your hands. It will be painful for a week at least, so keep taking the painkillers.'

The nurse handed her a leaflet.

'We recommend that all burns sufferers read this. Even after the wounds have healed the shock can cause emotional aftereffects. This gives you a list of support groups. Patients tell me that it really helps to talk to people who have experienced similar burns however they were caused.'

Chapter 7: Corrosive Secrets
How do I understand this woman?

Adrian was fuming. He wanted to let out his anger but not at Precious even though he was furious with her. How could he avoid it? He went to the gym and took it out on a punch bag. As he walked home he tried to organise his thoughts and to work out how to tell her without making things worse.

'She kept the threats a secret from me and now she doesn't want the acid attack to be reported but I'm a journalist. She doesn't get how all these secrets exclude me. Does she want me in her life or not? Am I some kind of ornament? That's what feminists say a lot. I'm being unkind but I need to get these poisonous thoughts out of me if I'm to be of any use to Precious in her recovery.

After their meal that evening Adrian could contain himself no longer.

'After Nairobi you promised to have no more secrets from me!' he said through gritted teeth.

'I wanted to tell you, Ade. I really did but it was all happening when George was ill. I told you about the attack in the garden didn't I? With all the pressure you were under and the grief, I wanted to spare you more anguish. I promise you, it wasn't because I didn't WANT to tell you.'

'Why weren't you getting witness protection?'

'We thought they didn't know where I live now and I don't think they do know. The second time the guy must have followed me from the meeting. Drawing attention to where I live could have upped the risks. It'll all be over soon anyway.'

Adrian ate in silence, conscious that any confrontation could harm Precious when her nerves were already so frayed. Despite his quiet demeanour his mind was in turmoil. He was at a loss to understand this woman, whom he thought he knew. But she'd kept so many secrets from him for so long. What else hadn't she told him? As a reporter he was no stranger to the impact of crime but his involvement stopped after reporting it. He was trying to think his way through the attack on Precious.

He argued with himself.

'What kind of man am I that I can't protect my wife? I love her to bits and need to help her through this but how do I control my anger? If she's going to have secrets she keeps from me, how long can our relationship last?'

He broke his silence to ask,

'When are you going to call Nechesa and let her know what's happened?' asked Adrian.

'I don't want to worry them Adrian.'

Despite all his efforts at restraint he couldn't stop himself – he snapped.

'You'll drive people away Precious if you keep having secrets. Do I mean so little to you that you felt you needn't tell me about the threats? And now you don't want to tell your sister even after she's been so close to you? She's been there for you at the hardest times in your life. What does this say about you? '

Precious started to cry; the first time she had cried since the acid attack. Adrian's expression softened. He regretted what he had said but at the same time felt glad he'd said it. Suppressing it had made him behave without spontaneity.

'You're right Ade. I'm not a good wife. For ten years I've only been accountable to myself. You had so much to cope with and I didn't want to add to it but I was wrong. I'm sorry. And you're right about Nechesa, too. I shouldn't behave like that to her either. The time spent alone together at my father's funeral made me realise what a great sister she is. You must think me some kind of loner.'

'We've both lived on our own for years – it'll take time.

This isn't going to be easy but having secrets will drive us apart. It could even kill our relationship. My job is words but I'm not good at expressing what I feel about you. All I know is that love should give us courage and strength and if you don't want my love you have to tell me. '

His voice had become tender and he started to massage the back of her neck. Precious looked up at him and said

'I do love you. I do, I do, I do.'

'You're the best thing that has happened to me. I don't want to keep calling you Precious even though you are. When we are alone together I'll call you "Ebony" like the colour of your hair. You think of a name for me. Let's create new identities, just for when we are alone together, and promise never to have secrets from our new selves.'

'I love that idea Ade. The first time we slept together, you looked to me like a bear sated on honey. I'll call you "Bear".'

∞

When the bandages were taken off for the last time she looked at her hands. Stiff but no longer painful; they were so ugly. Every time she looked at them she would be reminded of that act of revenge. How was she going to cope with that? Precious was afraid and she couldn't comprehend the whirling myriad emotions ready to explode. She needed help. She looked at the leaflet they had given her at the hospital. There was a group who met in Ealing – a few stops from Shepherd's Bush. She arranged to go to a meeting. When she arrived at the house she realised it was also the office of Southall Black Sisters. She got to know them when she first arrived in England and lived and worked at the Women's Refuge.

She guessed the reason why they hosted this meeting. Many of the victims of acid attacks were sufferers of domestic abuse. The most common cause was when a rejected boyfriend or divorced husband was determined that their ex should not be attractive to other men. The circumstances of Precious's attack were unique in the group. Given that, she was unsure how helpful this was going to be.

One thing she felt immediately was gratitude – gratitude to Delroy. His warning had saved her face. Many of the women in the room must once have been stunningly beautiful. Some still were because they had trained their hair to hide most of the damage.

Through the door arriving a little late was Jean. Despite the damage around her eyes and she had obviously lost sight in one, Precious recognised her. Jean had been a resident at the hostel. She had a vibrant personality and had helped to keep the atmosphere almost cheerful.

Precious stood up and greeted her.

'Jean, it's been a long time.'

'You are the last person I expected to see here. Do you remember how we called you Sister Precious because you seemed to us like a nun who'd taken a vow of chastity? Our jokes were not always kind but we couldn't imagine you getting hurt as you seemed to avoid men.'

'Oh Jean. I'm married now but my husband didn't do this. But it wasn't an accident either.'

A bit like in Alcoholics Anonymous Precious had to tell her story.

Jean said, 'Winter is coming and it may help you to begin with to wear gloves and it won't look strange. There are thin skin-colour gloves available which you can wear for dances and social occasions but you will become less self–conscious and feel less need for them.'

'What is your story Jean? When we last met you were planning to move north to try to start a new life and resume your nursing career away from Ryan.'

'He found me the week before I was due to move. Since

then I have worked for Southall Black Sisters. I wanted to help other women avoid what happened to me. At least Ryan went to gaol. Working here has been my way of not being a victim Precious. You'll come through this, I know you will.'

'Your reaction reminds me of my reasons for joining the police. It was the last thing Katie expected me to do. I certainly didn't come to this country with that in mind.'

'So why did you join?'

'Katie and I were travelling back to London after a day out in Brighton. The train kept emptying until, besides me and Katie, there was only an old gentleman and a group of white youths. There must have been about eight of them, boys and some girls aged between 14 and probably 18.

'We were minding our own business chatting away when suddenly being black I attracted their attention. They started making rude gestures and monkey noises and they got louder and louder. At first we tried to ignore them but they kept moving closer and closer. Then one of them leant over me and put his angry face right in front of mine and shouted,

'Stop staring at me, you orangutan.'

'So what did you do?'

'I froze in my seat, but Katie stood up and said calmly to the boy, "How dare you call my friend orangutan." But that didn't calm the situation instead the boy picked up the fire extinguisher and threatened to spray both of us.'

'When it looked as if they were about to carry out their threat the old white man sat in the corner stood up. He told the boys he couldn't sit there and watch them treat us like that and therefore he pulled the emergency chain and the train stopped.'

'My God, then what?'

'We sat there for about fifteen minutes but it felt like an eternity. The train driver came to find out why someone had pulled the chain and the lovely man explained. The train driver said "In that case a crime has been committed and I am calling the police."

'And did they come?'

'Yes they did and this is where it gets interesting. Two white police officers one male and one female spoke to everyone in the carriage including the boys. They took our names, addresses and telephone numbers and moved the boys into an empty carriage. They said they would contact us for further questioning, but they didn't and they didn't appear sympathetic to us. They seemed more concerned about the few passengers left on the train whose journey was interrupted. A year later that boy committed a more serious crime. This time a young woman was badly beaten but she was afraid to testify. Only then did they knock on my door to ask me to attend an identity parade to identify the boy with the fire extinguisher.'

'So it was because of this incident that you went to work for the police?' asked Jean.

'Yes. After that experience I understood why Africans who have been here longer than me don't seem to absorb themselves in society, but instead go to African churches, African shops and societies.'

Precious and Jean hugged, and Precious said she would come again. When she got home she told Adrian about it

'It's been good for me. If I can find comfortable gloves then I'll use them because I won't be staring at the scars every time I'm on the computer. Seeing them makes me re-live what happened. Jean is probably right – as time passes I might not need them so much.'

'Sounds like a good idea.' Adrian held her hands and gently kissed them. 'To me everything about you is beautiful.'

'My soppy ol' bear. What would I do without you? Some of those women are too afraid to try another relationship. And the man has to be pretty special in the circumstances.

I'm lucky having you and lucky that my face was spared. The MET gave me so much support. Ade, most of the men who do this sort of thing get away with it but the guy who did this to me is in prison awaiting trial.'

Precious clenched her right fist and jabbed it in the air then sighed.

Chapter 8: The Trial
Overcoming fear

Precious kept herself busy so that her nerves surrounding the trial were kept at the back of her mind, only reappearing in her dreams, where faceless figures threatened her and Abeo's lifeless body lay in her arms.

The days leading up to the trial put a huge strain on Precious and Adrian. Precious grew more and more apprehensive about appearing in court. After the acid attack could there be more? The attackers intended to frighten her into withdrawing her evidence. Every time Adrian tried to talk about it, she changed the subject.

He wanted to be there for Precious, a friendly face amongst the press. As part of the agreement with the paper, Adrian could cover the trial and The London Post would publicise the Abeo appeal. Adrian knew that, whatever he did, nothing would make it easy for her.

Nowadays, this volume of coverage of a trial only happened when the case was of national interest. Despite being a graduate recruit, when Adrian started his career he was treated like any other green reporter and sat through trials and London County Council meetings. Adrian reflected that it had been good training because even the most sensational trials had boring bits where maintaining attention was not always easy.

It was 6 am on the day of the trial. Adrian watched as Precious read her statement over and over again. He couldn't be angry with Precious for long. He dragged himself out of bed and offered to go through her evidence with her. She was grateful but with Adrian's anxious gaze on her she felt even more emotional and barely held herself together.

It was not the first time Precious had given evidence but this case was different because it was so close to her heart.

The loss of a boy she'd known meant she couldn't summon up professional distance. The threats had made her nervous but she vowed that she wouldn't allow herself to break down in court, not in front of Abeo's family.

She showered and dressed carefully.

'What do you think?' she asked Adrian. 'Appearances are so important in court. I must look immaculate and everything about me must be pristine.'

She looked down at her well-polished shoes and adjusted her scarf.

I've been over and over my statement but I don't feel prepared, Ade.'

She trembled at the thought that her evidence could mean that Jacob and Nelson would face life behind bars if found guilty.

'Believe me, you look perfect, 'said Adrian. 'I'll be a friendly face in the public gallery and I'll have an artist with me sketching. I'll ask him to make one of you.'

On the journey to the court she couldn't help remembering when she'd last appeared with a colleague in court. As PC Andy was being cross-examined, his almost undetectable stammer had come to the fore. It had been terrible watching him struggle as words wouldn't come out of his mouth, sometimes not at all and occasionally not as fast as the prosecutor had expected. She'd thought of it as *'Eshirimi'*. As a child she had been taught that if some stranger hid in the dark and scared you it could affect your speech for the rest of your life.

Giving Evidence

As Precious entered the court room, her eyes were drawn to Abeo's parents and the familiar faces of the mourners she had seen at the church service before Abeo's body was taken back to Ghana for burial. Everyone looked solemn. She was surprised to see that the twelve members of the jury all looked white and middle class apart from one man of South Asian ancestry. Precious wondered if they could have a good grasp and understanding of this case? She reserved her judgment and wished for the best – a fair trial.

'Precious Harris, I believe you are a civilian trainer employed by the Metropolitan Police. Is that correct?

Precious simply said, 'Yes'

'You were off duty at the time that you witnessed the murder of Abeo Amah? Is that correct?'

'Yes Sir. That is correct. I am the founding chairman of Crossroads, a charity which works on the Wentworth Estate, and I was on my way to a meeting of trustees in the community centre.'

'You were the last person to see Abeo alive. Can you describe for the court what happened?'

'I travelled to the Wentworth Estate by tube and had just walked past the new library when I heard Abeo calling to me. '

'What did he say? '

'He just waved, smiled and said 'Hi Miss' – I was not married at that time.'

She glanced up at the public gallery and caught sight of Adrian taking notes.

'How did you know Abeo and can you tell the jury about him?'

'I came to know most of the young people on the estate through working with Crossroads. The majority of children over the age of eight have been involved in our activities at some time. There were only a few who showed no interest.'

She glanced at the defendants.

'Once you met Abeo you were not likely to forget him. His curiosity was irrepressible and he enjoyed study and above all loved reading, particularly non-fiction. I remember on a similar occasion seeing him on his way to the library to return some books. I asked him what he had been reading. He showed me books about astronomy and the history of space exploration and immediately started to describe what he had read. He was a teacher's dream pupil: bright, interested and a quick learner.'

'What happened on this occasion?

'I watched as he skipped by in the direction of the library. It was Thursday and open late. I continued on my way to the community centre. I had only gone about a hundred yards when I heard a scream. My instinct made me turn around and shout "NO!" as I ran back in the direction of the library. Abeo was lying on the ground blood pouring from him.'

'As I approached Abeo I heard a voice I thought I recognised laughingly call out "Serve him right, the little African shit." I saw two boys running across the road and disappearing down Chapel Street. I knelt beside Abeo, took off my scarf and tied it tightly around his waist to try and stop the bleeding. I whispered, "Stay with me please, Abeo. Look at me. Say something. Please talk to me." So yes, I was the last person he spoke to but all he was able to say was "Miss…", and then he was gone.'

'But you are sure that there were two of them?'

'Yes, and not just me. The young man who called the ambulance also saw the two teenagers run away.'

'It was the combination of hearing him curse, his height, his physique, his clothes and the way he moved that all pointed to it being Nelson. He always wears a red bandana around his neck and carries a small Gucci man bag.'

'No further questions your honour.'

Then it was the turn of the defence barrister:

'So Mrs Harris, you are good at recognising people from their back. I put it to you that lots of boys in this age bracket wear bandanas and carry man bags. As these are so common you cannot be sure that this was Nelson. The person you saw was not Nelson.

'No sir, I am certain it was.'

The barrister handed some photographs to the usher.

'Your Honour, I would like to introduce some photographs for the witness to look at. I have copies for the jury and your honour. There were four photographs of the backs of four black teenagers.

'Two of these pictures are of Jacob and Nelson but which ones? Would you kindly tell the jury?'

Precious looked hard at the photographs and hesitated. All four boys were dressed the same and had similar haircuts. She felt her chest tighten as she realised she couldn't be certain. She looked at the judge.

'Your honour, these boys are all dressed the same. On that night the boys were moving. These four are all standing bolt upright. I wouldn't like to say which are Jacob and Nelson.'

"You wouldn't like to say" and yet you accuse these boys of murder?'

Precious felt the blood drain from her face.

'That is all, Your Honour,' said the defence lawyer as he sat down with a satisfied look on his face.

Precious left the witness box with a heavy heart. She had let everyone down. Why couldn't she have seen their faces? As a key witness had she done enough to convince the jury so they had no doubt about the identity of the perpetrator? Precious couldn't look at Abeo's parents, whom she felt must be overwhelmed with emotions hearing again what had happened to their son, and how he died.

She left the court forgetting that Adrian was there. He knew she would be upset so hurried after her and met her on the steps outside. His proud African Queen looked utterly defeated. When she saw him she said, 'Take me home, just take me home.'

Adrian hailed a taxi and they drive home in silence. She couldn't bring herself to speak about it.

∞

Adrian was back in court in the public gallery in a seat reserved for the press. As a witness Precious would have to hear from him second hand the account of what happened next.

The Prosecuting Counsel stood up.

'Your Honour, I wish to make an application in the absence of the jury.'

The jury filed out of the court.

'Your Honour, new evidence has just come to light and I wish to call a witness to the crime.'

'There has to a good reason to allow him at this late stage? '

Counsel for the Prosecution continued,

'A gang member witnessed the murder but has until now kept it secret because he is frightened for his life and his family. Something snapped inside; he was sick of all the knifing and killing cutting short the lives of young people he knew. He felt he could stay silent no longer but he would like to testify nameless. He has been offered special protection as a key witness.'

The jury was summoned to hear the evidence of the seventeen-year old. He walked into the witness box with a confident swagger but his eyes betrayed the fear inside. Beads of sweat appeared on his forehead as he took the Bible to give the oath.

'I saw what happened; I saw Nelson pull a knife and stick it in Abeo's chest. I ran after them down Chapel Street. I heard Jacob say that they wanted to teach him a lesson for grassing. They didn't mean to kill him.'

The defending counsel tried his best to destroy his credibility suggesting that he was from a rival gang trying to get revenge. The witness stayed calm and didn't lose his temper and looked as if he was only able to do that because he was telling the truth.

'Why should the jury believe you? You have admitted that you have taken part in gang activities and have left it late, too late really for the defence to mount a proper examination. I ask the judge to adjourn.'

The prosecution defended the witness vigorously.

'Your Honour, it has taken witness X a great deal of courage to come here today. Fear for his own his life held him back but now he regrets that. I would like to ask the jury to look at him as I ask him again if he witnessed the murder.'

He walked towards the jury and said, 'Look at him and make up your own mind. Decide for yourself if he is telling the truth?'

The judge instructed the witness.

'Look at the accused please and point to the one who you saw put the knife in Abeo.'

Witness X pointed straight at Nelson.

'It was him, Sir.'

Adrian was able to tell Precious what happened next. Jacob agreed to become a witness for the prosecution in exchange for a lighter sentence. He had not wielded the knife. The jury found Nelson guilty of manslaughter; they accepted that he had not intended to kill Abeo.

The Aftermath

Adrian's articles in the local and national newspapers following the verdict were received with wide acclaim. Thanks to his editor's support, he was able to expand the scope of the articles and encompass wider issues. He was keen to capture the underlying racial and cultural tension in urban London and bring understanding to people unaware of the pressures affecting young people.

Adrian wrote what people were thinking but not saying: in London the main problem is black-on-black violence. But instead of solely blaming the black community, he examined knife crime in other cities with different racial profiles but with similar problems of social exclusion, and boys knowing little beyond their few square miles of territory.

Adrian examined how gang culture created a climate of fear and a need to keep safe, even if that meant carrying a knife. Many young people thought it was the only way to survive. And how could you blame them, when they'd been groomed by the 'survive or die' atmosphere? The article crossed age, culture and ethnic barriers.

'There is hope.' wrote Adrian. 'Glasgow ruled out a 'WAR on drugs' as the means of tackling their epidemic of white knife crime. Judging it 'a health problem' has reaped enormous success. The causes were similar, so why not try the same remedy in London? It's not a case of black or white.'

Precious put down the paper and looked proudly at him.

'How are you able to do that? You see the reality I glimpsed when I arrived here seeing London through the eyes of a foreigner.'

'In truth, Precious, I couldn't have done it without you. I wouldn't have become involved in Wentworth without you. But there is something I haven't told you.'

'What's this? Are you keeping secrets from me?' grinned Precious.

'I suppose I'm guilty too. The truth is that I've met Nelson before.'

'What! And you never told me.'

'Maybe I shouldn't be telling you now, but I thought you should know after the trial. An unusual child-law firm of solicitors in Brixton held a competition in the local schools on the subject of The Empire Windrush, and I was asked to cover it. I wanted to write about their work as well. They explained to me what it involved. They had cases where children had been removed from abusive or neglectful parents. Nelson was one of them. His father was absent and his mother had periods of addiction following domestic violence so Nelson was taken into care. But the state is often not a good parent either. It's good at looking after physical needs but not emotional ones. I noticed him because he was so angry. At aged ten, he was already being groomed by gangs. I compared him being taken from his mother to the loss I felt after my mum died. After hearing that kind of story I remember thinking that I'd never feel sorry for myself again.'

'I assumed he must've had a disrupted childhood,' Precious said after a long pause. 'Happy children don't go round stabbing their peers.'

Adrian agreed. 'But at least with the Abeo Foundation you've got an opportunity to make the difference with some kids, even if you can't save everyone. Could you take the Abeo trustees on a trip to Glasgow? See how they have tackled these problems? The paper might let me go with you.'

'How can I do everything? I need to start work on George and Kioni's charity. I feel like I haven't even begun the planning for Abeo's fund, and on top of all that I'm still working full time. I feel like I'm fighting fires but no matter what I do, everything is burning.'

'I wondered about that, too.' confessed Adrian. 'We have the funds from the house to pay for George and Kioni's project, but this one is different. The donations from the newspaper mean that we will have the money to pay someone to coordinate the Abeo foundation. If you want, you can take a step back from that.'

Precious looked unsure. 'I can't do that. I couldn't tell the Amahs, "I'm sorry, but I don't think your foundation is worth my time".'

'You can't do everything, Precious' Adrian said firmly.

'You'll be no use to anyone if it carries on this way. You need to decide what is most important to you, but something has got to give.'

Precious knew what was important to her. The charities were what she truly believed in, and where she felt her time would be best spent. If the work at the Abeo foundation was paid, she could afford to quit her job and focus on the task full time.

'I have to quit the police,' she said firmly. 'If I have Delroy as my deputy director, I can split my time between the two charities.'

'You want to run two charities at the same time?' Adrian replied in disbelief. 'That's no mean feat.'

'I know, but it's worth it. I need to do it. I have to help.'

∞

The project paid for Joshua Amah's plane fare so he could be present at the launch of the 'Abeo Africa-Caribbean Friendship Foundation'.

The plans for the house conversion were approved. They appointed a local building firm to project manage it, but even so they needed to attend consultation meetings about what they wanted. The pace of their lives was intense while Precious worked off her notice.

On her last day, her colleagues threw her a farewell party. 'It's not goodbye is it?' She said to her gathered co-workers. 'The Abeo Foundation will mean that our paths will cross a great deal.'

She grinned at Sergeant Jones, 'To those of you celebrating seeing the back of me, I'm sorry, but I'm not going anywhere soon.'

That night an exhausted Precious switched off her alarm and was surprised when she slept dreamlessly until eleven the following morning.

Chapter 9: Construction
Building a new life

Adrian and Precious moved back into the Shepherds Bush flat while the builders converted the Notting Hill house into flats. It was what George wanted, but it felt like traces of his life were being demolished bit by bit until the house became a shell. Precious felt that her life was being remade too. Adrian had been right, splitting her time between two charities was not easy. She felt like she was being pulled in two opposite directions and she didn't know how much longer she could cope.

Adrian's piece on the trial had brought in even more donations and the campaign had raised £400,000 in total. He was energised by his heightened career and came home enthusiastically talking about an interview with the Home Secretary. He poured drinks for both of them while Precious served up the veggie chilli she'd cooked. Her arm hit the glass of red wine and it smashed on the floor.

As her gaze swept over the fragments of glass spread across the floor, she felt that she was peering down observing her life shattered into pieces. She frantically looked for the dustpan and brush whilst tears pressed against her throat and she felt a wave of hysteria. An impossible sound of laughter and crying escaped her throat.

It was too much work. Both projects deeply touched her and she felt honoured to the tips of her toes by the confidence shown in her, but she didn't share that belief in her abilities. She had been wrong believing she could do both. Taking on two new challenges felt overwhelming – she hadn't the time or the resources to do a good job for one, much less two. It was a lose-lose situation. And whenever she tried to point that out to people, they kept patting her on the back and telling her how amazing she was and how she could do it. No one believed her. She really couldn't.

Adrian knew this was not about the broken glass. She was struggling with the responsibility and fear of failure but he suspected that, after the trauma of the trial and being assaulted meant supressed feelings were behind it. Adrian worried that it could be PTSD. He told her to sit down while he cleared up the mess.

To lighten the mood, Adrian tried a kitsch Egyptian dance as he brought the food to the table. 'I like your new style, my Egyptian queen.'

Angry tears appeared in her eyes. She stood up and started to yank at the braids with a ferocity that disturbed Adrian.

'Stop! What are you doing?'

'Why? After spending all afternoon in the hairdressers just to be mocked by you after I've cooked you dinner?'

'It was just a joke to change the mood. I wasn't making fun of you. I don't think I'll ever understand you, Precious.'

'Sure! We savage Africans are so hard to understand.'

'F'ck. That was uncalled for Precious. You know that's not what I meant.'

Precious could see that was true. Why had she reacted so angrily?

'I'm sorry, Ade. You're right. That was unfair. Everything's too much at the moment. I'm not coping, am I?

Precious let him kiss her and attempt to put her hair back in place. Later, when she'd had time to cool off and relax they tried a more serious conversation.

'Precious you will succeed—I know you will—but you have to think of yourself too. Delegate what you can, but you need a break—some thinking time. We haven't even had a proper honeymoon.'

She looked grateful but exhausted.

'How can I take any time off?'

'On Sunday, we'll head for the South Downs and take a long walk to clear our heads.'

The Long View

Once at the top of Butser Hill, they sat down and took out their thermos. While they sipped the comforting Kenyan coffee, they took in the view of the A3 snaking through the valley below, the South Downs and the English Channel in the distance. White clouds raced across the sky over the ancient landscape—a meeting of longevity and change.

A sudden energy claimed Precious.

'I have an idea. I'm looking at a landscape I've not seen, but I feel connected to it by this taste of home. What if we can somehow connect the Abeo Foundation to our Kenyan project? I'm not sure how but I have this feeling that connecting them is what is needed and maybe a taste of Kenya is what will make it happen.'

Adrian had no idea what was in Precious's mind but felt relieved that her positivity and energy had returned.

Chapter 10: Ten months later
The key of the door

Adrian's optimism was returning. Precious was beginning to put the trial behind her and had thrown herself into work for the Abeo Foundation. He jangled the keys. He wanted to surprise her. The builders showed him around the completed house. If it didn't have the same number on the door, he wouldn't have recognised it as his teenage home. He called in an estate agent to value the penthouse apartment, which they intended to sell to fund the Kenya project. He couldn't believe the amount. It was as much as he had earned in journalism in total since leaving LSE. What a strange world where property was more valuable than people's talents and efforts.

Adrian handed Precious the key to their flat.

'Wow. Is this really the same house, Adrian? It looks like something out of Grand Designs.'

Precious took off her shoes.

'I don't want any dust on this beautiful floor.'

Adrian kept his shoes on.

'Come on, let me show you around. I'm glad you like the oak floors. They are easy to clean. We need to buy stuff. We'll have to leave most of our furniture in Shepherds Bush to let it furnished.'

The living area was open plan and double doors led into a bright conservatory. On either side of the wide passage leading to it were three bedrooms, two with en-suite bathrooms. Adrian opened the largest one last. Precious expected it to be empty so she gasped.

'When did you do this?' She asked as she bounced on the king size divan with a deep mattress.

'Won't Nechesa just love this! This bed is like the one in

the hotel.'

The wardrobes were fitted and unlike the other rooms with their polished floors this one had a deep white carpet with flecks of beige.

'I hope you don't mind,' said Adrian. 'You can choose the furniture for the rest of the flat but I wanted to surprise you.'

'You've certainly done that. You are quite the magician, my bear. I'm going to rename you *Aladdin*.'

'In that case I'm going to wave my magic wand because I have a wish to make. You know what I want, don't you?'

Precious allowed herself to be undressed slowly by Adrian just as he had on their first night together. When they fell laughing onto the bed she was totally aroused.

∞

A few weeks later they were able to move in and put the penthouse flat with its roof garden up for sale. It was not long before the estate agents received offers. After exchanging contracts, Adrian and Precious went to celebrate and they messaged Nechesa saying, 'Not long now!'

Chapter 11: Plans

Nechesa:
How to understand the past in order to build a future

The proceeds from the sale of the Notting Hill flat were deposited in the trust account and Precious was busy every day phoning and emailing Nechesa to check up on the organisation of the building.

'When do you have to be back in Uganda? Can you stay until the centre is built?'

'I resigned from my post months ago but don't be concerned – I've applied for a headship and have been short-listed. They want to interview me. If I'm appointed I need to go back before the beginning of the academic year but that leaves me almost three months. I've asked my girls to come here when university breaks up next month. Rachel and Rose can help and the experience will be good for them.'

∞

Kioni and baby Joseph came out to meet Precious when she arrived in Tusanda. After giving her daughter a big hug and a glass of water, Kioni wasted no time. 'Come come, see the land we have bought.'

Her daughter was impressed. The location near the primary school was perfect and a hundred yards away was a field they could cultivate. Precious and Nechesa worked together to finalise the plans and employ the builders. When Precious left for England the foundations were already dug: Nechesa was proving to be a capable project manager. She estimated the structure would be ready in two months. Kioni oversaw the planting of the small holding where they could grow crops to feed the orphans. Even at 81 she wanted to get her hands in the soil.

Precious heard the murmurs of disapproval suggesting

that Uncle Moses should be in charge. It was completely unacceptable for men to have to take orders from a woman.

'Don't worry, I've a thick skin,' said Nechesa.

'Remember that he who pays the piper… and in this case it's *she* who pays!'

'You wouldn't have said that a year ago. You've changed Nechesa. What's happened?' asked Precious.

'Come on. Let's get some coffee. I'd like to talk about it.'

They took a thermos to their favourite place by the river.

'Remember that day we helped Osundwa sort through father's papers? Reading about the fifties and all the suffering made me think: Why didn't we know about it? Over one hundred thousand died: either killed or starved or became sick in the camps. And all the militarised villages!'

'You're right. Not just here. Adrian was shocked. He's a well-informed journalist but even he wasn't aware of the extent of the oppression. He felt ashamed of himself because he had bought into the idea of Mao Mao being barbaric.'

'When I was in England do you remember we went to see that film 'Suffragette'? Why is it people have to make such sacrifices to make the world a better place and then those of us who enjoy the benefits forget all about them?'

Precious had never heard her sister talk with such passion.

'Our people know nothing about it? Don't you think they should? Why don't they know? What is the reason that the men who have power in this country don't want them to know?'

'I don't know the answer, Nechesa, and I don't quite know where this conversation is leading.'

'After all that sacrifice Kenya deserves to be a better place. When I was in London, I talked to Adrian about it. He told me about a court case demanding compensation for Kenyan veterans of the British army like Uncle Peter who were detained and tortured. They were given compensation totalling £20m. Why don't our leaders demand compensation for the others as well?'

'I don't know, Nechesa.'

'Look, we both admire Wangare Mathai. Rose teases me that I go on about her too much. Looking at your face, you probably agree with her. Yet it was you who used to sing her praises.'

Precious grinned and waved her sister on.

'Wangare was prepared to suffer and be tortured like those suffragettes. You remember that her life was threatened. Sure she wanted to protect the environment but she wanted to empower women too. She said that even a woman without any wealth could plant a tree and make a change.'

'You are right, Sis. She deserved her Noble Peace Prize', said Precious.

'You asked me what's different about me. Well I believe that this country will only change if women change it. We need confidence if we are to create a dynamic economy and the most entrepreneurial people I know are women but they aren't supported.'

'You need to leave teaching and go into politics.'

'It's tempting but I wouldn't last long, would I?' Nechesa grasped Precious's damaged hands.

'Even worse could happen to me if some of the men in power think their power is under threat.'

'I'd like to build an enterprise but I don't know how so for the time being I'll stick to education. But this experience you've given me is prompting ideas so you never know where this will lead me. Thank you Precious. This wouldn't be happening without you.'

Precious hugged her sister and the warmth spread through her body and her brain.

London

On her return Precious caught up with Delroy. She could never meet him without looking at her hands. She had so many reasons to be grateful to him. She looked on him like an adopted father.

She was as impressed in the change in him as she had been with her sister. With money from the Abeo Foundation, Delroy had expanded the Crossroads activities in music, drama, martial arts and yoga to engage more young people on the estate. He'd been taken aback by the success of the poetry rap class led by a charismatic teacher.

'I don't have to tell you that incidents of mental illness in young people are rising, but I've witnessed some moving sessions. Maybe just talking about it in whatever form is a kind of therapy. It's helping a lot of disturbed kids.'

'The performance of our version of 'West Side Story' went down a storm. Maria was played by Kezia who is part African and Tony was played by Ismael whose parents are from Guyana. You know what our problem is?' said Delroy.

'I think I know what you're going to say. We're reaching young people with motivation but not those who've been excluded from school.'

They decided to erect a summerhouse in the repaired garden where the truanting children, mostly boys, could hang out. It became a place where Delroy could meet and mentor them. Bit by bit over the next month, he broke down barriers, but even so they presumed Precious was joking when she said she wanted to take five of them to Kenya. Once she persuaded them that she was serious they took notice.

She suggested that if they were really interested, they should come to a Crossroads Club and discuss it. It had been a while since Precious had attended a club night and she was overwhelmed by the welcome from the members for her and the boys.

Not everyone was interested in chatting but about fifteen gathered around her.

Little John piped up. 'Miss, tell us about Africa. Is it like what we see on comic relief? Why do babies have a sad look and faces covered in flies?'

Precious smiled,

'Where I come from there is nothing like that, people have dignity and are just like the people we see in Wentworth just getting on with their lives.'

'Eh! Have you seen that dude what's his name, Lenny Henry in your village?'

Delroy laughed and Precious looked at Sam, Goldie and the others.

'These guys want to come with me to Tusanda to decorate the Education Centre we are building. Will you help them raise money for their trip so they can take photos and report back?'

Fay, who tended to be shy and reserved, disappeared into the club kitchen and returned with an old empty biscuit tin they'd been using for storage. She dropped in her only pound and rattled the tin.

'Spare change, spare change, please,' she called as she went around the room collecting the little coins from everyone's pocket.

'Come on Fay!' exclaimed Sam. 'Do you know how much it costs to fly to Kenya? That won't even get you on the tube to Stratford.'

'Well, you have to start from somewhere.' replied an unusually confident Fay.

At the end of the meeting the youth leader counted the coins and to everyone's amazement they'd raised £20.

'What a start, guys. This is a great idea. Perhaps we could have weekly meetings and come up with ideas about how we can raise the money.'

After the enthusiastic session the boys were up for the trip, but Precious issued a warning.

'It'll be an adventure for you but not a holiday. You'll work harder than you have in the whole of your life. So, if you want to come with me you have to be fit and wake early in the morning. That means no truanting and good behaviour in class. If I hear a bad word from your teachers then I can't take you. You'll also need to raise some of the air fare yourselves and not rely on the others to do it all for you.'

Precious liaised with the head master at their comprehensive school. As long as the boys were not disruptive they could return to school and their names would go in the hat and five would be chosen. The mufti day to fundraise for them raised over £1000. Sam and his mates looked moved and, for the first time in years, they felt like they belonged in school.

'Better than thieving, miss,' he grinned.

Precious told them that the local Rotary Club had promised to double every pound raised. It was going to happen. It had felt like some kind of fantasy, but now they punched their fists in the air in excitement. Then the reality sunk in. This was serious.

Their task would be to paint, decorate and put finishing touches to the day centre. Local builders and decorators offered to give them tips. Precious couldn't believe her luck when one of them, Lendon Graham, who had come over from Jamaica aged ten, volunteered to go with them.

'I didn't know my Dad when I came over and he wasn't much of a father really,' Lendon told Precious. 'I rarely saw him but I was lucky because my mother married Harrison. I was pretty sulky and rebellious at first, but he took me fishing and to the football which was cool. Once he had my attention, he taught me my trade. My success in business is thanks to him. Most of these lads just need someone to teach them some skills they can be proud of and to praise them when they do something good. To feel loved and appreciated is what these boys need.'

'I agree' said Precious, 'but they have to be honest about the things they've done if they want to change their lives.'

Chapter 12: Female Empowerment
Rap is not just for boys

When Precious called in at the jam session at the community centre she discovered that news of the proposed trip to Kenya had spread. Four girls were rapping together. Precious was impressed by their ability to connect, harmonise and react to each other. She was taking it in when they spotted her. A mixed-race girl grabbed the others and said,

'Let's move it and jam somewhere else. We aren't her top boys.'

Precious went after them and said,

'Tell me. What's the matter?'

'You know what's the matter,' said Jill. 'You're taking some of the Wolf Crew hangers-on to Kenya. Is that what we have to do to get opportunities? Truant or get excluded from school? Do you have to be black and male? What if you are white, brown, Chinese or female like – squalay it's not for us?'

Precious sighed, 'I understand but can we have a coffee or an ice cream and talk, please.' They agreed.

'You're right, and once the Tusanda Education Centre is up and running, I promise I'll organise a trip for you girls. Do you think you could get a group together who could do a sponsored climb of Kilimanjaro? You'd have to train hard and it's not an easy climb.'

The girls responded enthusiastically.

'Can it be a co-ed group?'

'Of course, if that's what you want. After the climb I'll take you to help in the centre, but it needs establishing first. You do understand why I'm taking those lads? I have no idea how else to bridge the gap between them and African immigrants. I want a taste of Africa to open their hearts.'

Jamila looked at the others.

'Maybe we can help? How about we put on open music sessions? Encourage Afro beats as well as Caribbean and rock and rap. Make a small charge towards our Kilimanjaro fund? You are serious about taking us there?'

'Of course I am, but you need to be a little patient. It may take a year for me to organise it properly. Is that okay?'

'We'll need that time to train and raise the money,' said Jamila.

When Precious arrived home she told Adrian about the girls.

'Rewarding good behaviour makes sense,' said Ade. 'But you've no choice but to inspire those boys otherwise they'll end up in jail like Nelson and Jacob.'

Precious was thinking hard about what to do. She thought of her young self and her lack of opportunities because she was female and felt a wave of guilt.

Chapter 13: Transported
Stars in their eyes

Precious had a change of heart and included Jamila and Miriam in the group who would decorate the day centre. She promised the other girls that they would definitely go with her on her next trip. Adrian intended to join them six days later ready for the grand opening.

'I wouldn't miss it for the world,' he said as he kissed Precious on her way.

∞

When they exited Nairobi airport Declan, the youngest in the group, looked surprised.

'I can't believe it. They have nice cars and roads.'

'Idiot! How did you think they get around?' said Sam loudly.

Miriam looked none too pleased at Sam's remark.

'Know it all! You'd know a lot more if you hadn't skipped school so often.'

Sam quietened down.

Jamila's grandparents had fled the war in Uganda during the dictator Idi Amin's time.

'This is eerie. I've never been to Africa but it's exactly like how my parents described it.'

Miriam's parents were originally from Trinidad. As she looked out of the bus she said, 'Thanks for bringing us, Miss. This opportunity means a lot to me. My brother's green with envy.'

It was getting dark when they arrived at the village. Most houses didn't have electricity. Sam looked at the sky. It was a shocking black out experience but awe inspiring.

'Man look at those stars, ain't that something!'

After a hushed welcome and a quick meal, they all went to bed and slept as only teenagers can.

The following morning, they woke to the most beautiful sunrise they had ever seen. They were given a tour of the village of the kind Adrian had enjoyed. The villagers stared but also smiled and some banged drums in welcome.

When they reached the river, Sam tried jumping to the other side rather than use the stepping stones. He didn't quite make it, and the Londoners and the Kenyans couldn't help but laugh as he shook the water off himself like a dog. Sam took it in good spirits and threatened to shake even more next to a shy Tusandan girl and Miriam. The Tusandan girl looked surprised as Miriam chased him. As they walked to the village centre Nechesa half whispered to Precious,

'Do you remember that afternoon when mum started chasing us when she saw us talking to the local boys? We'd just come home from school for our summer holidays and these two boys started talking to us over the fence, we couldn't help but agree to meet them the next day by the river.'

Precious started to giggle.

'I know what has brought this on. One of those boys tried to jump across the river and ended up in the water as well.'

Nechesa started laughing.

'Mum didn't like us hanging around with local boys in case we got pregnant. What did she think? Pregnant by osmosis? Talk to a boy and you're pregnant.'

'Do you even remember the boys' names?'

That set Precious off.

'Of course not! Mum never gave us the chance.'

The pair fell into a comfortable silence as they watched the children messing around in the road, occasionally shouting at them to get out of the way as a motorcycle zoomed by. They kept catching snatches of conversations. Mainly teasing and joking.

'I feel like I'm hoooome,' Jamila shouted as she ran past them.

'You're not from Kenya, you're from Uganda – idiot!' said Miriam as she chased after her.

'Still better than Trinidad,' Jamila shouted back.

'No it's not, Trinidad's the best!' Miriam said and the two disappeared down the path bickering happily.

∞

Nechesa had organised an opportunity for some Tusandan boys and girls to meet the Londoners. They had never met white teenagers before and they were excited. Nechesa prepared a set of ice breaking exercises to get the group going but also topics to help them compare their lives in Africa and UK.

When the day was coming to an end, Nechesa summarised by thanking them all for taking part but said,

'I'm amazed by what you have discussed. So many of the same issues have come up whether you are from rural Kenya or from London.'

They all just wanted to feel safe, loved and accepted by their peers, family and society. But there were significant differences too. The Kenyan youths felt education was the only way out of poverty whilst the UK youth didn't think about education as the only way to succeed. Most of the Kenyan youths had lost both parents from HIV/Aids and lived with relatives whom they were so grateful had taken them in, whilst the Londoners barely knew anyone in the family who had died apart from either their old grandparents or some young person who had been stabbed for being part of a gang.

The Kenyans were speechless when Sam described the appeal of the gangs on Wentworth estate. They couldn't understand why anyone would want to be part of a group that would put them at risk of death? This was beyond their comprehension. They didn't know why anyone would kill another young person for no reason. They had only seen such stories in films and couldn't stop asking questions.

∞

After the orientation and planning of the activities for the week, the seven Londoners were assigned groups with a clear plan of daily tasks, followed by reflections of their experience before bedtime. They were reminded of the need to look after each other, something alien to them. Despite the few fall outs on their arrival they had realised that it was the best way to survive the challenge ahead. They must work as a team, support each other and learn how to talk in public every evening during reflection time. The tone was set on the first night.

'I don't feel I'm being judged, or have to be with someone else or keep watching my back in case I'm a target,' said Julius.

'I love this place,' nodded Sam.

'Boy did you say 'love'. Ugh that's not like you Sam.'

Sam gave Julius a punch, a playful one.

A feeling of friendship and trust was in their grasp.

'Stop it you two!' said Jamila. 'I want us to be serious for a few minutes. Did you meet your Tusandan namesake Sam? I went with little Samuel to his house, if you can call it that. There's a hole in the roof, the floor is muddy and he doesn't haven't shoes. What are we going to do about it?'

On the second day the group got stuck into painting the centre. Kioni thought orange and black would stand out and thanks to Nechesa's organisation there was paint and brushes awaiting the workers.

At Jamila's insistence, Precious asked Lendon if it was possible to rebuild Samuel's house. She was unsure of the response she'd get, but he agreed to take two of the boys with him to take a look.

Using the boys and some local labour, it took only two days to rebuild the one-roomed house, but it meant working longer and harder than the London lads had ever done. When little Samuel and his family saw the sealed floor, the clean painted interior and the fine roof they wept with gratitude. The London boys looked subdued, almost embarrassed.

As they walked away Lendon slapped Sam and Declan on their backs in a congratulatory way.

Declan said, 'Who'd have thought that we could build a house? Back on Wentworth they won't believe it.'

Chapter 14: Transformations
The threat of educated women

The space started filling up with men, women and children, as they spread out from under the big Orembe tree which had been spared when the centre was built. Children surrounded Adrian, all tugging and pushing each other daring to see which one could sit the closest, chanting *'mzungu, mzungu'*, 'white man, white man' and reaching out to feel Adrian's hairy hands. He teased them saying *'habari'*, as the unexpected 'hello' came out of his mouth they scattered with fear, nudging each other. When he asked them, 'What's your name?' they just stared at him and giggled.

Behind him, Adrian noticed that just like at the funeral the men and women were separate. Precious had told him that usually the men do all the talking, but today they would break with tradition. Earlier she'd told him,

'This time Nechesa must start. Please encourage the children to clap enthusiastically. If necessary, tell them they'll get extra food if they do!'

Precious and Nechesa came out from inside the centre leading Kioni, who was to unveil the plaque. Nechesa took the microphone.

'Thank you all for coming to celebrate the opening of our wonderful new centre. It wouldn't have been possible without the help of my sister and her husband Adrian, who are here with us today.'

There was some polite clapping and enthusiastic drumming. Nechesa looked towards the visitors from London.

'They came bringing us extra joy and seven pairs of hands—no, eight.'

She smiled at Lendon.

'As well as working on the centre, Lendon has supervised some of our village boys helping them build enclosures for the animals we want to keep.'

Nechesa pointed to the outside of the building.

'Our English friends have decorated it for us inside and out. Please show your appreciation.'

The children responded just as Precious hoped. They would not go hungry!

'The person who recognised the need for this day centre is our wonderful mother and she has the honour of unveiling the plaque.'

Kioni walked gracefully towards the right of the main door. Precious handed her the ribbon to pull. Her mother struggled to hold back the tears as she said,

'It is my pleasure to open—' She gasped as she saw the name. 'The George and Kioni Learning Centre.'

The children and the women clapped but Uncle Moses looked angry. He summoned Precious, but she ignored his gesture as she set about explaining how the centre will work. After her speech, the doors were flung open for the villagers to take a look inside. On the tables was an array of food and drink. Adrian and the Wentworth lads had the broadest of grins on their faces and wasted no time in leading the children to the feast, like Pied Pipers. Nechesa led the women, pointing out features and describing what will happen where.

Precious went over to Uncle Moses.

'You wanted to speak to me, Uncle?'

'You should have named it after your late father. He was our respected senior chief of the Tanga people worthy of all the honour. I am sad and ashamed.'

Precious was silent for what felt to her like minutes, but was probably only thirty seconds, and then she could contain her thoughts no more.

'What did he do? It was Kioni who scrimped and saved so that I could get an education. Without that, the centre wouldn't have been possible and it was Kioni's idea, not yours and not mine. She shared the idea with my father-in-law and it was his legacy that has paid for it. Tell me, what had my father to do with it?'

Precious stopped and couldn't quite believe that she had talked so directly to Uncle Moses. He, for once, was speechless. She quickly excused herself and walked over to Adrian. He didn't need to ask. She sighed and told him what had happened.

'There are lots of Uncle Moses's in the world. He means well but his world is changing and he doesn't want it to change.'

They stopped talking as the one-eyed pastor from the local church stepped up to finish the ceremony and bless the building. He asked the chief's family to move to the front, because he wanted to pray for them as he closed the ceremony. He praised what Precious and Nechesa had achieved but her pleasure was quickly undone by his next words.

'These kinds of achievements are only achieved by boys not girls. Precious, you should have been a man. As a man you would lift this family and community out of poverty.'

In response, the women muttered to each other while 'mmmm's' spread in unison amongst the men and, unsurprisingly, Uncle Moses nodded in agreement. Then with a burst of joy the women raised their voices in a song of praise. Together they sung *'Mwana wamberi, Mwana wamberi ne shikhoyero'*, meaning 'my child has brought pride in the home' a song in praise and honour of what had been achieved by Kioni and her daughters. Kioni ignored the pastor's remarks as a sense of achievement overwhelmed her. Hearing the praise song, she recalled singing with the women over the years. Now a group of women had accomplished something most men thought was impossible. She has a big smile on her face.

Precious walked over to her mother. Kioni was shaking with emotion. She grasped Precious's hands tightly.

'You've fulfilled my dreams, my daughter.'

'No, Ma. You've fulfilled your dreams. I don't know how you did it. To think that you were born into a world where men determined your life, but you haven't let that happen to you or your daughters. None of this would have happened without you.'

After the crowd dispersed, Adrian congratulated Precious and she responded with an infectious, even triumphant, smile. It disappeared almost as suddenly as it had appeared and a serious and anxious look spread across her face.

'The women led by Nechesa are determined to play a bigger role, but I don't want to divide the family and my sister will have to return to Uganda. Uncle Moses upholds the old cultural belief of the importance of the difference between male and female. It's the past not the future. Tusanda will only prosper if the women are empowered. I see that clearly. Nechesa has been lecturing me about it. And look at her daughters. Given the chance they will be such good leaders. What can I do?

'Uncle Moses's entire life has been in Tusanda, under the big mango tree with my father as the patriarch. But Tusanda is just a small bush in this world and he needs to see beyond its branches. How can we help him do that Adrian?'

Before he could answer Precious found herself imagining life in his shoes.

'Even Kioni has seen London and he feels threated by educated women forcing change on the community. He thinks that means belittling him. How can I persuade him to embrace change and be part of it?'

Nechesa joined them and they began to discuss the

tragedy of the postcolonial world.

'The majority of people like Uncle Moses had no say in whether or not they wanted this new world. Men like him were not given the tools to negotiate modernity,' she finished.

As the evening drew to a close, Adrian and Precious made their way back to the house.

'Our discussion has given me an idea,' Adrian said. 'I was going to tell you on the way home when I hoped I'd have a clearer idea, but maybe this is the right time and place. I've been thinking of going freelance. Now my name is recognised, I can write opinion pieces. For that I don't need to work all hours on the staff at the paper. I want time to write a book. This is thanks to meeting you, Precious. You have a talent for taking people out of their old lives.

'I'll call my book *'Healing the Divide'*. It'll be a review of the difficulties confronting East and South African countries resulting from their colonial past. I want to write about Anvil. Most Brits have no idea of the scale and cruelty of the atrocities the colonial government committed and they should know. That will stop them saying 'Charity begins at home.' We owe reparations for the 100,000 who died in the camps. To have true healing and friendship we have to acknowledge the past and recognise how it's damaged people.

'You'll need to come here a lot, my Ebony. This way I can come with you, meet people, research and find non-confrontational ways to write about it.'

Precious looked stunned and held back tears as Adrian said,

'I'd like that very much. They say people don't change. Maybe their nature doesn't change but attitudes and opinions can change. A white boy growing up in Notting Hill Gate either lurched towards nationalist racist attitudes or, like me, took each kid as an individual. When I reviewed a genetics book I discovered I was right. Every human-being is unique.'

Precious looked thoughtful and replied,

'Mmm. You've transformed the house in Notting Hill but transformations can happen to people as well. If we could understand how it works we could change the world for the better.'

'You're right, Precious. It sounds simple and I wish it was. Not all the cynical journalist in me has evaporated – although you've done a pretty good job! What I hadn't realised until now was how my country's colonial past had affected even me. We're not good at seeing ourselves as others see us. I'm not a British version of Uncle Moses, but I'm beginning to understand why he clings on to what gives him pride.'

Precious's delight shone when Adrian made another suggestion.

'How about I talk to Uncle Moses and suggest that the village really needs a Health Centre? We promised to Whatsapp Osundwa to show him the new centre. Why don't we ask him to find the money for the Health Centre? After all, he's a rich enough American and is going to be chief one day. We could suggest that Moses do the planning in Tusanda? That way he becomes your friend and part of the project. What do you think?'

'Do it now please, Adrian, before the resentment sinks in.'

∞

That night when Adrian kissed her, he said, 'Congratulations, what an achievement. I'm so proud of my wife and now even Uncle Moses is on board. That will mean our time spent here will be so much more congenial. It will feel like home.'

'Thanks to you my darling bear, I feel confident that my times of panic are a thing of the past. Everywhere there is good and bad. Everywhere we will meet problems but I won't want to run away because home is where you are! You feel at home here and I feel at home in London. We can stride both places and make a difference in both. What more can we ask for? Except…'

Precious looked strangely coy.

'I need to congratulate you too.'

'I've done nothing,' said Adrian modestly.

'I don't know about that.' Precious whispered in his ear. 'I don't think the son or daughter of Adrian could have happened without you.'

The End

Reflections and Acknowledgments
(written by Sylvia Vetta)

The character of Precious is entirely fictional but the texture of her life is inspired by the life of Nancy Mudenyo Hunt. Nancy is the daughter of a Luhyia tribal chief and grew up in the area of Western Kenya where the African chapters are situated. She worked as a Leadership & Development Trainer for Thames Valley Police and with P.C. John Cornelius and P.C. Louise Russell she set up Exit 7 to transform the lives of hundreds of disadvantaged children in Oxfordshire. That experience and of founding and developing the Nasio Trust inspired *Not so Black and White.*

The origins of *Not So Black and White* go back to 2014 when Nancy Mudenyo Hunt and I first met. For sixteen years I was the chair of an organisation in my village called Kennington Overseas Aid (KOA). Every year, since 1969 the village had raised money for an overseas project, which we selected by vote. One of the projects submitted, by three charities for our consideration in 2014, was sent by the Nasio Trust. I loved the project but was not sure that it would secure enough votes to win because it took some understanding. The proposal was to raise £20,000 to build not a hospital ward or a pre-school, as we had done previously, but to construct tanks in which to grow an algae called Spirulina. The packed hall understood our motto was *helping people to help themselves.* The spirulina would not only provide a healthier diet for the 440 orphans fed at the educational day centre Nasio had built but would also produce quantities for sale commercially to help the project sustain itself.

The project was selected and Nancy and I met on many occasions during that year of fundraising events. At the end of the year KOA had raised £27,015. **So our first acknowledgement is to the residents of Kennington who**

supported the fundraising in 2014. Particular thanks go to **Halcyon Leonard** who was in the chair in 2014 and told me, 'I felt a special bond being Kenyan born.' Halcyon was also joint chairwoman with me in KOA's 50th and final year and has supported Nancy and me throughout our work together.

The project was delivered quickly and efficiently whilst also creating local employment. I realised we were working with an inspirational woman and I asked Nancy to join a select group of castaways whom I had sent to my mythical island of Oxtopia. For ten years *Oxford Castaways* was a monthly magazine feature published by *The Oxford Times*. In the interview I asked Nancy when and where she was born. Like Precious she immediately told me where that was but she also said,

"As a girl I was not valued — and that is probably why my father failed to register my birth. Some years later, my sister Betty decided that I needed a birth certificate and she registered me. She conjured up the date of January 10, 1970, although nobody knew for certain when I was born. So I have the choice of being either five years older or five years younger! I was named Ishmael after my grandfather, but Betty felt that I should have a girl's name and, on the birth certificate, I am Nancy Ishmael Ndula."

Two years later Nancy confessed that interview was the first time she had talked about her childhood to anyone. Out of that realisation developed the concept of the two main characters in *Not so Black and White.* Our next acknowledgement is to the then editor of *Oxfordshire Limited Edition* **Tim Metcalfe for allowing me to castaway Nancy Mudenyo Hunt.**

It is extremely rare for non- related people to write fiction. Collaborations in non-fiction are common but there are particular problems for fiction. There has to be just one voice and how do two people achieve that while writing together? We fleshed out the principal characters and knew how we wanted the story to end and the issues we wanted to tackle. So we made a start. I asked my friends **Dai Richards** and **Polly Biswas Gladwin** if they would read the first thirty pages and answer honestly whether it read as if written by two people. I knew that Dai and Polly would not hesitate to tell me if it was rubbish. When they replied liking it and saying that it read as 'one voice', the hard work began.

Fellow writers will know how many rewrites and revisions it takes **most** of us to get a novel to a publishable state. My first two novels *Brushstrokes in Time* and *Sculpting the Elephant* were published by Claret Press. Claret Press was prepared to publish this novel in late 2021/ early 2022. Then the world was hit by Covid–19. Nasio fundraising events were cancelled or postponed and Nancy and I felt that the proceeds from the sales should go to the Nasio Trust as soon as possible. Hence our decision to self-publish it as an ebook with the printed version to follow later.

Despite our decision to self-publish, both **Katie Isbester** and **Gina Marsh** of Claret Press gave generously of their time and expertise by providing thorough conceptual edits to set us on the pathway to write a compulsive read. Once we felt it had reached a publishable state we needed a copy edit. Nancy and I paid the modest fee asked by **Andy Severn of Oxford eBooks** to produce the book and Katie Isbester paid for the cover design but we couldn't run to a professional proof read. Among those who helped were **Jenny Forder, Marilyn Farr, Keziah Buss, Lucy Artus and Jack Brucker.**

We would like to **thank the artist Petya Tsankova** for the striking cover and **Adam Tarry** for the map of Africa

Our grateful thanks go to the **supporters of the Nasio Trust** without whom the projects which inspired this book would not have been possible. Thanks to **Marie Hooper** for her enthusiasm to market this novel on behalf of the Nasio

Trust. Nancy says, 'I would like to thank **my amazing staff in Kenya and the UK.** Without them there wouldn't be a Nasio transforming lives. And the children we support and the young people I have met over the years who have become family.'

On a personal note we would like to thank our family members for supporting us and particular thanks from Nancy to:

'My husband Jonathan Hunt and my two children Nigel and Chantelle for supporting me over the years. Love you all. x'

Thanks to all those who have read and endorsed *Not so Black and White.* Sylvia also wants to thank the **Oxford Writers Group** for their encouragement.

Glossary

Panga – Lupanga: A sharp metal tool commonly used for cutting undergrowth

Luhyia / Luo: Western Kenya tribes

Ugali: Bread made from maize flour – Staple food

Mzungu : a white person of European origin

Eshisira mbere: 'a verb used to warn ladies about men'

'Kata mumasika abaandu batsekhanga': a proverb meaning that during mourning people laugh

Wanjira: a go between during courtship that leads to marriage, usually an aunt related to the bride or groom

Matatu: a public means of taxi

Ishira: A negative repercussion to family members when one is involved in sexual activities outside wedlock

Mau Mau: – Muzungu Aende Ulaya Mwafrica Apete Uhuru – The white man must go back to Europe for the African to get independence. A liberation movement for independence in Kenya

Mwanawanje Omukosi: My beloved child

Appendix 3: Some Research

Letters, papers and pictures from Kenya 1952- 2000 from the records of Chief George Mudenyo, the father of Nancy Mudenyo Hunt.

The Wanga tribe of western Kenya inspired the fictional Tanga in NSBW

KING MUMIA OF WANGA.
PHOTO 1908 BORN 1849

Nabongo MUMIA - Chief of the Wanga Tribe. 1852 -1949

His parents were Nabongo Shiundu Wamukoya and Wamanya. Nabongo was appointed heir on the eve of his father's death. Mumia occupied a prominent place in British colonial administration from 1908 to 1926 and he was recognised as the Paramount Chief. He ruled the Kingdom for 67 years from 1882 to 1949 in one of the longest reigns in African history.

The Wanga Kingdom was the most highly developed and centralised kingdom in Kenyan history before the advent of British colonialism. When the British arrived in Western Kenya in 1883, they found the Wanga Kingdom as the only organised state with a centralised hereditary monarch in the whole of what later came to be known as Kenya. Mumia's royal background caused a dilemma to the colonial officers. He was "retired" by the colonial authorities in 1926, but maintained influence until his death on April 24, 1949. https://abawanga.wordpress.com/

Notes from the last decade of colonial rule in Kenya

Barbara Castle MP Tribune Sep 30.1955 (Barbara later became a cabinet minister in the government of Harold Wilson)

'In the heart of the British Empire there is a police state where the rule of law has broken down, where murder and torture of Africans by Europeans goes unpunished and where authorities pledged to enforce justice regularly connive at its violation.'

Duncan McPherson told Barbara Castle that conditions in the Kenyan concentration camps were worse than he had experienced in a Japanese prisoner of war camp.

Other Newspaper Articles:

Sydney Morning Herald – Salvationist Marries Blind Native https://www.nation.co.ke/news/kenya-blind-kimuyu-holloway/1056-5352216-l7lu1e/index.html
The Guardian: 'Love in Kenya. Problems facing mixed marriage
https://www.aljazeera.com/indepth/features/2016/04/mau-mau-kenyans-share-stories-torture-160428131800531.html

Books:
Britain's Gulag: The Brutal End to Empire in Kenya by Caroline Elkins
The State of Africa: A History of Fifty Years of Independence by Martin Meredith
Black and British: A Forgotten History by David Olusoga

Polemical but a thought provoking read: *Natives Race and Class in the Ruins of Empire* by Akala.

Some notable real life figures mentioned in Not so Black and White

Jomo Kenyatta
The First President of Kenya (1897-1978)

In September 1946 Jomo Kenyatta became leader of the newly formed Kenya African Union.(KANU) From the Kenya African Teachers College, which he directed as an alternative to government educational institutions, Kenyatta organized a mass nationalist party. On October 21, 1952, he was arrested on charges of having directed the Mau Mau movement. Despite government efforts to portray Kenyatta's trial as a criminal case, it instead received worldwide publicity as a political proceeding.

Kenyatta was released in August 1961, and, at the London Conference early in 1962, he negotiated the constitutional terms leading to Kenya's independence. KANU won the pre-independence election in May 1963, forming a provisional government, and Kenya celebrated its independence on December 12, 1963, with Kenyatta as prime minister. A year later Kenya became a one-party republic when the main opposition party went into voluntary liquidation.

Thomas Mboya (1930 – 5 July 1969)

Tom Mboya as he was generally known spearheaded the

negotiations for independence at the Lancaster House Conferences and was instrumental in the formation of Kenya's independence party, KANU which he served as its first Secretary General. He laid the foundation for Kenya's mixed economy at the height of the Cold War and set up several of the country's key labour institutions.

Mboya's intelligence, charm, leadership and oratory skills won him admiration from all over the world. He gave speeches and interviews in favour of Kenya's independence from colonial rule and spoke at rallies in favour of the civil rights movement in the USA. In 1958, Mboya was elected Conference Chairman at the All-African Peoples' Conference and was the Africa Representative to the International Confederation of Free Trade Unions (ICFTU).

Mboya worked with John F Kennedy and Martin Luther King Jr. to create education opportunities for African students; this effort resulted in African Airlifts of the 1950s - 60s, which enabled African students to study at US colleges. Notable beneficiaries of this airlift were Wangari Maathai and Barack Hussein Obama Sn. Mboya was shot dead by Nahashon Njoroge in 1969 who claimed he was employed by 'Big Men'.

Queen Elizabeth II (1926)

In 1952 Britain was starting to emerge from post-war austerity so Princess Elizabeth and her husband of five years felt they could embark on a holiday in Kenya. On February 6, they were staying in two room hotel called Tree Tops, a three hour drive from Nairobi, when Elizabeth was told of the death of her father King George VI.

In *Not so Black and White,* Kidake is due to fly to the USA to study when he learns of the death of his father and has to assume the role of chief. It was as if the fictional chief, like Princess Elizabeth, had his youth and freedom whisked away in a moment. On that day in Kenya her life changed forever. As we write she is Britain's longest serving monarch who has met and talked with not only all British Prime Ministers since 1952 but also, through the Commonwealth, the leaders of most countries that were once part of the British Empire.

Barack Hussein Obama Sr. (1936 - 1982)

He was a Kenyan senior governmental economist and the father of Barack Obama, the 44th president of the United States. He is a central figure of his son's memoir, Dreams from My Father (1995). Obama married in 1954 and had two children with his first wife, Kezia. He was selected for a special educational program sponsored by Tom Mboya and studied at the University of Hawaii. There, Obama met Stanley Ann Dunham, whom he married in 1961, and with whom he had a son, Barack II. She divorced him three years later. Obama went to Harvard University for graduate school, where he earned an M.A. in economics, and returned to Kenya in 1964. He saw his son Barack once more.

In 1964, Obama Sr. married Ruth Beatrice Baker, a Jewish-American woman whom he had met in Massachusetts. They had two sons together before divorcing in 1973. Obama worked as an economist with the Kenyan Ministry of Transport and was promoted to senior economic analyst in the Ministry of Finance. Obama Sr. had conflicts with Kenyan President Jomo Kenyatta after the murder of Tom Mboya which adversely affected his career. He was fired and blacklisted in Kenya, finding it nearly impossible to get a job. Obama Sr. was involved in three serious car accidents during his final years; he died as a result of the last one in 1982.

Mary Leakey (1913 -1996)

The British paleoanthropologist discovered the first fossilised Proconsul skull, an extinct ape which is now believed to be ancestral to humans. She also discovered the robust

Zinjanthropus skull at Olduvai Gorge in Tanzania, eastern Africa. For much of her career she worked with her husband, Louis Leakey, at Olduvai Gorge, where they uncovered fossils of ancient hominines and the earliest hominins, as well as the stone tools produced by the latter group. Mary Leakey developed a system for classifying the stone tools found at Olduvai. She discovered the Laetoli footprints, and at the Laetoli site she discovered hominin fossils that were more than 3.75 million years old. During her career, Leakey discovered fifteen new species of animal and also brought about the naming of a new genus. In 1972, after the death of her husband, Leakey became director of excavations at Olduvai. She maintained the Leakey family tradition of palaeoanthropology by training her son, Richard, in the field.

Wangari Maatai (1940 – 2011)

Wangari Maatai is an activist in the causes of development, democracy, peace and protection of the environment. She achieved many 'firsts'. Wangari was the first African woman to receive the Nobel Peace Prize (2004). She was also the first female scholar from East and Central Africa to take a doctorate (in biology), and the first female professor ever in her home country of Kenya. She founded the Green Belt Movement in 1977 which by the early 21st century had planted 30 million trees.

Wangari is quoted in Not so Black and White in the prologue saying that to plant a tree you don't need government permission. That planting just one tree empowers the individual and that individual can be poor and female. She is mentioned many times in the novel inspiring the main character particularly because of her role in female empowerment.

Barbara Castle (1910-2002)

This British example of female empowerment is only

mentioned once but we quote her at the beginning. She was one of the most significant Labour Party politicians of the 20th century and developed a close political partnership with Harold Wilson and served in several Cabinet roles during both his premierships. As Minister of Transport (1965–1968) she oversaw the introduction of permanent speed limits, breathalysers and seat belts. As Secretary of State for Employment and First Secretary of State (1968–1970) she successfully intervened in the strike by Ford sewing machinists against pay discrimination – a film Made in Dagenham featured the story. Following this she introduced the Equal Pay Act 1970.

In Britain she was a fine example of an empowered woman but she was also an internationalist aware of the crimes of Empire. She was unusual in 1955 in trying to publicise what was happening in Kenya ' In the heart of the British Empire there is a police state where the rule of law has broken down, where murder and torture of Africans by Europeans goes unpunished and where authorities pledged to enforce justice regularly connive at its violation.'

Barbara Castle MP Tribune (Sep 30.1955)

That awareness was clear in her first cabinet post as the first Minister for Overseas Development, a newly created ministry for which she had campaigned.

Appendix 4:

About the Nasio Trust and how you can support it.

Founded in 2001 by Nancy Mudenyo Hunt, her husband Jonathan Hunt, Helen Lord, the late Mark San and Lillian Osore.

Nasio Trust is a UK and Kenyan registered charity which feeds, educates and provides healthcare for orphaned and disadvantaged children in western Kenya. All aspects of a vulnerable child's life are covered, by supporting their emotional, physical and psycho-social development through access to education, emotional support, advocacy, food security, health and welfare services and community strengthening. Through supporting children to adulthood in their communities, rather than in an institution, they are enabled to reach their full potential and able to support themselves and their families. This method is geared towards breaking the cycle of poverty and enabling the communities to be self-sufficient, helping to eliminate the need for reliance on external funding.

While working for Thames Valley Police in 2001, as a leadership and development trainer, the idea for a programme to help young people in Oxfordshire who had lost direction was born. Nancy, with police colleagues, Louise Russell and John Cornelius developed a unique programme for young people called Exit 7, culminating in volunteering at the Nasio projects in Kenya. This life-changing programme has taken over 200 young people to Kenya, some of whom were disadvantaged or otherwise vulnerable. The connection between two very different communities had a profound effect on the Oxfordshire young people, changing their lives for good. Although the events in this book are fictional they relate to real life issues that affect both communities today. Read more about how the charity began and what it is now doing at http://www.thenasiotrust.org

Other Books by Sylvia Vetta

Sylvia Vetta is best known in Oxfordshire for her long running *Oxford Castaways series.* Nancy Mudenyo Hunt was one of the inspirational people she sent to her mythical island of Oxtopia along with inspirational objects, art and books. The 120 interviews were turned into three books. https://www.youtube.com/watch?v=ea-viXdvSm4

Sylvia's first novel *Brushstrokes in Time* (Claret Press) set against real events in China was inspired by another castaway. The artist Qu Leilei was a founder of the courageous Stars Art Movement (Beijing 1979). The Meridian Society made a series of video interviews about the book. It has been published in German as Pinselstriche https://www.facebook.com/TheMeridianSociety/videos/1141067562675489/

Her second novel *Sculpting the Elephant* is also published by Claret Press and is set in Oxford and India. As in *Not so Black and White* there is a multi-racial love story but it also explores lost history. https://youtu.be/d_H2CY5upUM

To see all her books go to https://www.sylviavetta.co.uk

This photograph of Nancy with the NatWest 2015 Award for most Inspirational Woman was taken by Helen Peacock.

A note from the chairman of the Nasio Trust

Having spent my career in the justice system I recognise all too well the issues covered in this book. Since retirement I have been chair of the Nasio Trust and witnessed not only the profound impact the charity has had on the people of an area of extreme poverty in western Kenya, but also the transformational change the experience has had on young people who visit the project. Nancy richly deserved the Honorary Doctorate she was awarded by The Open University for her exceptional contribution to development and social exclusion.

Keith Budgen CBE, Chair of the Nasio Trust

www.thenasiotrust.org
Breaking the Cycle of Poverty

Lightning Source UK Ltd.
Milton Keynes UK
UKHW011824230720
367020UK00002B/38

9 780995 543515